Starting Again

Cjaye Kendall

www.cjayebooks.co.uk

Starting Again

Copyright © Cjaye Kendall 2011

This novel is entirely a work of fiction. The names, characters and incidents portrayed in it are the work of the author's imagination or used fictitiously. Any resemblance to actual persons, living or dead, events or localities is entirely coincidental.

All Rights Reserved

No part of this book may be reproduced in any form, by photocopying or by any electronic or mechanical means including information storage or retrieval systems without permission in writing from both the copyright owner and the publisher of this book.

ISBN 978-0-9568359-0-1

Cover Design by Justin Scott

First Published 2011 in the UK by Cjaye Books

Printed and bound in Great Britain by 4edge Limited

In memory of

Mamma and Pa, Who love me and are proud of me, just for being me.

Also in memory of Nanny, Mavis and Evelyn.

Thank you

Angie, Justin, Susanne and Dave H.

Also thank you to everyone else who has helped me along the way (you know who you are).

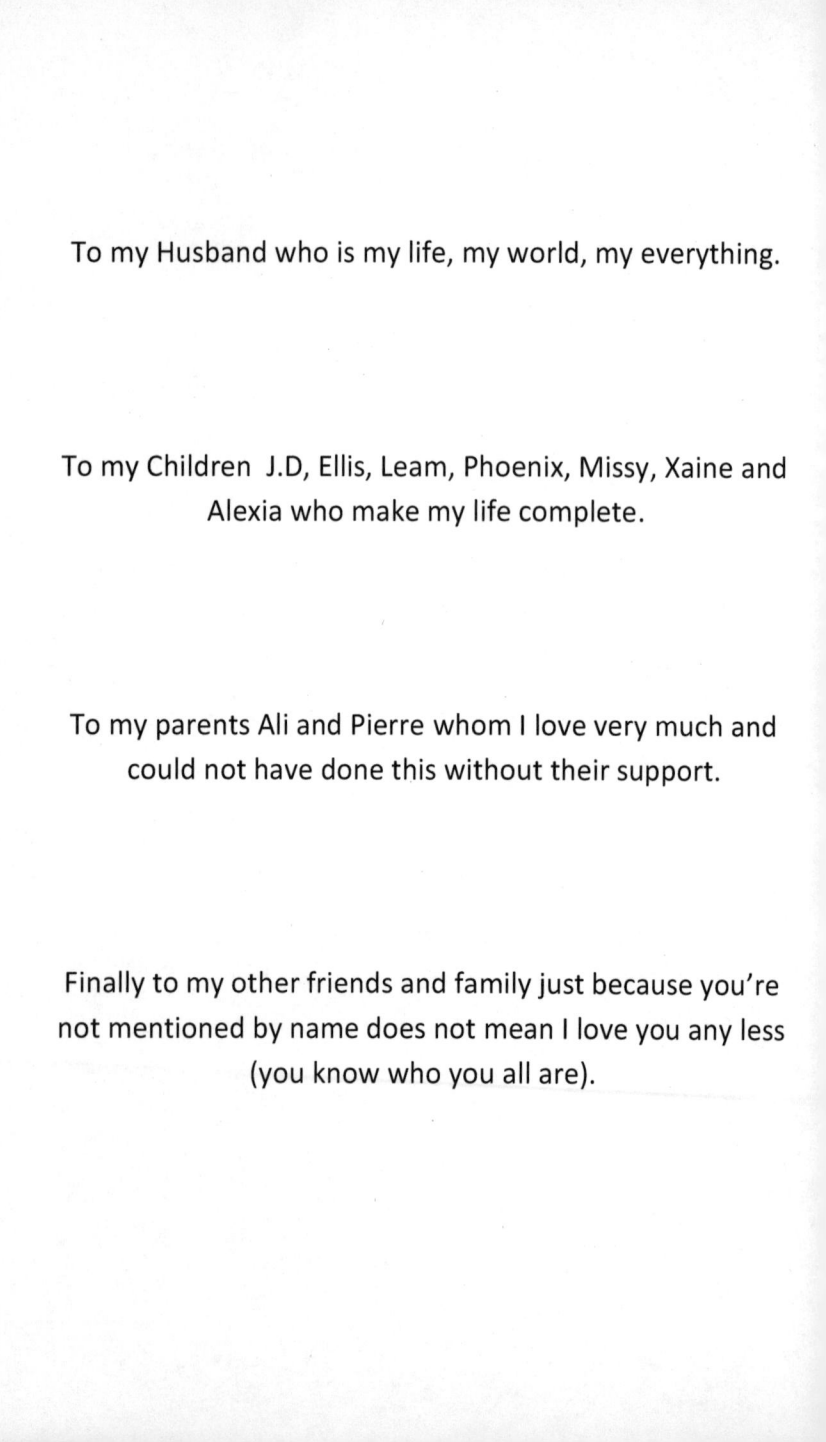

To my Husband who is my life, my world, my everything.

To my Children J.D, Ellis, Leam, Phoenix, Missy, Xaine and Alexia who make my life complete.

To my parents Ali and Pierre whom I love very much and could not have done this without their support.

Finally to my other friends and family just because you're not mentioned by name does not mean I love you any less (you know who you all are).

Starting Again

Cjaye Kendall

Prologue

Annette had met Simon during the summer when she was just seventeen, she was at college studying an interior design course and Simon was four years older than her. He rented a flat owned by the company whom he worked for, she moved in with Simon at his insistence. After six months she fell pregnant with Daniel. Shortly after that, at Simon's request she gave up college, they'd had a quick non fussy wedding, a small family affair with just her parents, her best friend Maddie and some work friends of Simon's.

The pregnancy was an easy one, no morning sickness, no swollen ankles, just a touch of heartburn every now and again, nothing a good swig of heartburn remedy did not resolve. Daniel's birth was an easy one, just five hours labour, during which time Simon never left her side, he reminded her to breathe at all the right times and pant when she needed to, with one final push and a final crushing of Simon's hand Daniel was born. Simon was the first to hold him, he cut the cord and even shed a few tears.

Simon's work relocated them north to Scotland when Daniel was six months old. Annette had left everything behind; she had left all her friends and family. Simon had talked her into it and he painted her a perfect picture of their new life, nice big house with a large garden for their children of whom Simon had planned three, two boys and a girl, the family dog a golden Labrador, and both of them still head over heels in love living the perfect life.

Chapter One

Annette relied on Simon for everything, he was loving and really attentive of her. The house was a reasonable size with a small garden for Daniel to play in "just a stop gap" Simon would tell her. When they first moved Simon was the most wonderful, loving husband and father you could ever wish for. Annette believed in the perfect family life Simon had painted for her, he used to let Annette have a lie down when he came home from work, at which time he would do the housework, look after Daniel, bathe him and then wake Annette gently in time to give her son a kiss goodnight. Simon used to love putting Daniel to bed that was his job as he had normally left for work by the time Daniel had woken up in the morning so he made up for it in the evening. Annette had regularly rung her parents and her best friend Maddie to tell them how wonderful Simon was and how happy she was and how their life really was a perfect life.

By the time Daniel had started nursery at three years old Simon had begun to change, Annette was no longer telling her family and friends about her perfect life, in fact she was avoiding talking to them at all, and when she did, she made sure the conversations steered towards whatever the caller was doing or had done rather than about herself.

Simon had started to drink every evening before coming home from work, "Just a couple of pints" he used to say when he rang her. The pressures of work Annette told herself. He always eventually arrived home albeit hardly able to walk and had missed Daniel's bedtime by hours. His behaviour and moods had started to change too, if Annette mentioned to him she'd had one of the other mother's from nursery around for a cup of tea he used to fly off the handle, rant and rave about the state of the house and how could she even think to have anyone around with the house looking like a bomb site.

Annette could never understand this, the house was not perfect but it was always clean and tidy, so she started making more of an effort and would clean and scrub as long as she had the hours to do so.

Annette used to regularly call her best friend Maddie, the only friend she had left from back home, Simon did not really like her having Maddie as a friend he thought she was a bad influence on Annette. Maddie herself was still living a young, free, single life. Simon did not want Annette getting ideas that Maddie has a better life than they had themselves. Maddie was just a slag as Simon used to call her when Annette dared to mention her name.

Annette used to look forward to hearing where Maddie had gone for the weekend and more importantly with whom. They used to giggle as Maddie retold her stories and described her latest dates, the latest one who apparently looked like someone from a 1970's rock band; he had described himself as having "short hair" in the lonely hearts advert, when he really meant "Bald". Annette deep in thought pondered why Simon never really liked her having friends, but just thoughts were where they stayed, it was easier to keep quiet than to argue her side and start Simon off on one of his rants.

By the time Daniel had started infant school two years later, she had stopped inviting other mother's back to her house as it was not worth the aggro from Simon, she wondered to herself, when at her loneliest if she would ever get the pet dog she was promised for company, the days were so long now she was all on her own in the house. Of course Annette made damn sure she had the house tidy for when Simon came home plus his dinner ready in the oven, but still the sarcastic comments came when "the dog" was mentioned. Most evenings Simon would fall asleep on the sofa in front of the TV after eating his dinner and knocking back a few more whiskies or beers depending on how much of a bad day at work he'd had. She now only really spoke to Maddie once every couple of weeks or so and her parents she spoke to even less than that. Simon used to complain that she had done nothing all day other than natter away about pointless shit to her friends or her mother and father, he used to check the phone bill when it came in to make sure she had not spoken to them any more than the agreed once a fortnight, "To save the phone bill getting too high" he once said when she finally plucked up the courage to ask him about it.

Six months went by with this daily routine of Simon coming home, dinner ready, house clean and tidy, Simon falling asleep on the sofa and empty beer cans or whisky bottles for Annette to clear up in the morning. Simon started coming home at 11pm every night smelling of perfume, if Annette ever dared question why, Simon answered "The barmaid in the pub just gave me a hug goodbye, what's the problem with that?'

One year he had even forgotten their wedding anniversary, Annette had cooked a lovely meal she had spent the day slaving over cookery books and recipes and running around the shops finding the vital ingredients.

She put Daniel to bed early and had Simon's present on under her new dress she was wearing, she had left a message on his mobile telling him not to be late and she was really excited to see him, she had planned a special anniversary evening for them which she had told his answer phone. By 9pm she had given up and had eaten her now cold dinner, by 10pm she had cleared his plate away, by 11pm she had gone to bed throwing her new underwear in the wash basket, hanging the dress she had bought back on the hanger and back in the wardrobe, by midnight she had fallen asleep fed up of trying his mobile which was switched off smugly announced by the female voicemail she thought. At 2am she awoke as Simon stumbled through the front door and dragged himself up the stairs into their bedroom, he stunk of alcohol and that same perfume again, Annette sat up in bed she'd had enough that was the last straw! Her eyes red and puffy from crying herself to sleep, she yelled at him, demanding to know where the hell did he think he had been, demanding to know what the hell was going on. He slurred a confession, an affair with the barmaid or "he'd been shagging the fit barmaid" as he put it, who had apparently been all over him for months and that's where he had been and who with, he begun taunting Annette saying how much slimmer and prettier the barmaid was compared to her and told her there was nothing she could do about it.

Oh yes there is thought Annette as she turned and faced a drunken swaying Simon she shouted 'I'm leaving you, you bastard, how can you do this to me?' 'To us!' she finally shrieked.

She marched into Daniel's room tears welling in her already red swollen eyes, she was determined not to let Simon see how much he was hurting her, she bent down to pick up a sleeping Daniel out of his bed, she was going to bundle him in the car and drive to her Mum and Dad's house, even if the final destination was eight hours away she knew what she was going to do.

As she bent down to pick Daniel up out of his bed Simon was right behind her with one quick, silent motion he grabbed her by her hair and pulled her away, she went to scream her heart pounding with fear, Simon held his hand over her mouth and dragged her back into the bedroom. Annette was in shock, all the anger and determination she'd had suddenly gave way to pure, terrifying fear.

Simon threw her on their bed cruelly taunting her that she was a bad mum for almost waking her son in the middle of the night, how she was a useless wife who never gave him what he wanted and he was never going to let her leave him and warned her if she tried, he would kill her. It was at this moment she noticed the look in his eyes and knew immediately he meant every word he had just said, in a flash he had punched her hard in the face, hard enough to make her nose bleed, she went running into the bathroom and cried. Eventually she had stopped the bleeding and had cleaned up the resulting red stains around her, she then looked in the mirror her face was pale, her nose was swollen and she had the early signs of bruising appearing around her left eye. She walked back into her bedroom still shaking with shock and fear and wondered if it was all just a bad dream. Simon was asleep on top of their bed, face down in the pillow, still with his clothes on, if it was a dream it really was not a good one.

In the morning when Annette awoke, Simon was standing over her, she shrank back in to the covers and cowered away from him, he bent down towards her, Annette's heart was pounding, she wondered whether to scream or not. Simon got closer she could feel his breath on her face, just as Annette opened her mouth to scream he flung his arms around her and said how sorry he was, and set about promising her the world and how he would no longer drink in that pub, he also promised to stop seeing the barmaid. He said it was just a drunken kiss and begged Annette to forgive him, he explained how the barmaid had come on to him and above all he said how sorry he was for making her cry and messing up their anniversary. He never mentioned the nose bleed or black eye and she was too scared to ask why.

After that night for almost a year he came home straight after work and he no longer smelt of drink or cheap perfume, Simon was once again the man she had married,

Annette had begun to think that the perfect family picture Simon had painted so convincingly was starting to take shape, Simon was making her cups of tea, taking her and Daniel on family days out and one night he had even surprised her by saying he had arranged a babysitter and was taking her out for dinner, just to show her how much he loved her and it was a late seventh wedding anniversary treat. Annette was excited, they had celebrated their seventh wedding anniversary a few months ago with a take away and a film, nothing special as Simon was too tired after work, but this *was* going to be special. Annette had a long soak in the bath with a splash of baby oil, shaved all the bits she could have done and put on the new underwear she had put away last year, satin knickers and pale pink satin bra to match, she painted her fingernails and toenails to match the underwear and then slipped into her favourite little black dress, she was surprised she still managed to fit into the dress, she also wore a light pink cardigan as April in Scotland was not the warmest of months, but Annette had wanted to look good.

The last time she had worn the dress Daniel was four years old, she had worn it when Simon had taken her to her favourite restaurant as her birthday treat, but Simon had got drunk and had ruined that evening. Annette pushed all those thoughts out of her head, tonight was going to be good, she and Simon were back on track, they would have a great meal and he would finally get to see the new underwear, they would make love when they got home, soft, gentle and slow. She could not wait to feel Simon's strong arms around her and the feel of their skin on each others. They had not made love in ages, Simon was normally too late home or was too tired, Annette never pushed the subject but she knew tonight would be the night, the best night they'd had in ages.

Annette had gone downstairs when the doorbell had rung, the babysitter had arrived and the cab was due any minute, she walked downstairs as Simon opened the front door he turned and watched as Annette stepped down into the hallway, 'You look stunning' he told her with a smile, 'You don't look to bad yourself' grinned back Annette.

They went to a quiet little restaurant in the middle of town, Annette had never been here before, the lights were dim and candles were on the tables, white tablecloths and leather padded chairs, they had been shown to a nice table for two by the waiter, Annette smiled and said thank you as the waiter pulled out her chair and placed a napkin on her lap.

Annette picked up the menu and wondered what to order, but before she'd had a chance to peruse the delights in store, Simon had whisked the menu out of her hands, he said he would order for her as it was his treat. He beckoned the waiter and ordered one Ravioli with goats cheese and a red pepper sauce for himself and soup of the day for Annette's starter, for the main course he went on to order, spring lamb noisettes with rosemary cream, roasted seasonal vegetables and a creamy mashed potato for himself, for Annette he ordered her a green salad with no dressing, she thought to herself she would have preferred the lamb but did not want to spoil the evening, as always Simon did know what was best for her, she did not want to behave like a spoilt child by demanding to have what she wanted. She sat back in the chair and looked over at her husband. He was six foot tall, with brown hair, blue eyes and he was clean shaven tonight, he was wearing a maroon shirt that complimented the colour of his eyes and black trousers, she looked at him and her heart swelled, she loved him, she truly did and everything he did was for the best for her, Daniel and for them as a family. Annette had married him for better or for worse, the evening was still going to be a great evening. Annette was picturing him lying next to her with no clothes on, his hand running over her breasts, she normally just laid on her back staring at the ceiling when they did get around to doing anything other than sleeping in their bedroom, she was used to telling herself it would be over soon and with a final grunt a drunken Simon would roll off her and fall asleep leaving Annette wondering if this was what the rest her life would be like, even with joys of these last few months she was used to comforting herself with the thoughts of it just being the pressure of Simon's work, and when work settled down in a few months he would be 100% back to being the loving attentive husband he used to be, but the worry for Annette on that thought was that she had not fully seen that side of him for some years now, although slowly in this last year or so he was coming back to her bit by bit, day by day and tonight was *the* night she reminded herself as she ate her salad. Dinner was finished off with a couple of coffees, cream and sugar for him and black for her at Simon's say so. Simon drank his coffee down in almost one, paid, and swiftly grabbed her by the arm and pulled her into a waiting mini cab; she never had a chance to finish her coffee. He would not talk to her during the cab ride home, she tried to snuggle up to him on the drive home but he shrugged her away, for the rest of the journey her excitement turned to dread and she replayed the whole evening in her head wondering if and when she had said or done something wrong. They got home and he sent Annette upstairs to run him a bath she heard him thank and pay the babysitter, she breathed a sigh of relief as he sounded calm and jolly she even heard him laugh at something the babysitter had said. Daniel was sound asleep in his bed, it was his seventh birthday soon and they were both taking him to the zoo for a family day out, Annette had tiptoed in and given him a kiss on the forehead and then went to run the bath, Simon came in the bathroom behind her and shut the door, Annette grinned to herself, she turned around to pull him close to her so she could kiss his neck the way he liked it, she knew tonight would be the night, she looked into his eyes but saw his blue eyes blazing with anger not lust, like she had expected. Annette was scared, very scared, her heart was pounding in her chest she tried to back away but had nowhere to go, he raised his fist, she tried to shield herself with her hands, wondering what was going on, he brought his fist down to the side of her face, he was yelling that she was a tart, a slag and a whore she tried to ask why but no sound came from her mouth, she tried to push him away but she was not strong enough, she thought she heard screaming, she realised it was her who was screaming, he was hitting her again and again with blows to her arms, her legs, he was shouting about the waiter and how she was giving him the eye, the come on and how embarrassed he was by her, she really was trying to get away she hit out at him, he grabbed her arms and dug his fingers in, why did she think a young waiter would even find someone as fat and ugly as her attractive in the first place. Finally he let go of her arms, grabbed her by the hair and threw her on the bathroom floor, he gave her one last kick and said he was going to bed, as he turned around and opened the bathroom door he looked at Annette, a bruised, bleeding, crying heap on the floor and growled, 'Now look at what you made me do you stupid bitch. Clean up this mess, don't you ever do any housework you lazy bitch!'

He walked out and shut the bathroom door behind him without a backwards glance.

Annette was finally alone she heaved herself to a sitting position on the floor and looked around her, the bath was overflowing, towels were strewn all over the floor, the bubble bath she had been holding in her hand had dropped to the floor at some point and had splattered all over the bathroom, the mirror was broken, he had punched her so hard into the wall where it hung the back of her head had smashed it, Annette was bleeding, bruised and crying, she rubbed the back of her head where a large lump had formed and she looked at her dress, it was ruined and ripped, her new bra strap and been torn away from her shoulder which was cut and bleeding, she hugged herself and cried. She must have cried herself to sleep on the bathroom floor or passed out due to the shock and pain. When she awoke she was still in the bathroom, cold and wet, her head was throbbing and her whole body was sore, she heard the front door slam. Simon must have left for work; she guessed it was around 5am the time he normally left. She heaved herself up and begun very slowly and stiffly to tidy the devastated bathroom, she wanted it done before Daniel woke; she really hoped he had not awoken and heard anything that had happened during the night.

She tidied the bathroom and went into her bedroom. It smelt of Simon she ran back to the bathroom and threw up.

'Mum are you in there?'

Daniel was knocking on the door.

'Yes love' she croaked back.

'Will be out in a sec, mummy's just not feeling too good.'

She unlocked the door and Daniel stared at her in horror, she had a big bruise to the side of her jaw, a bruised swollen nose and a black eye, then Daniel looked at the wall behind her.

'What happened to you mum?' he noticed the broken mirror and frowned.

'I slipped over and landed face first into it' Annette said, it was the first excuse that had come into her head.

'Oh silly mummy' he said giving her a hug.

'I wondered what all the shouting was last night, I was scared so I stayed in bed and hid under the covers, I should have come out and helped you up mummy' he said in a quiet voice, 'was daddy very cross you broke the mirror, was that why he was shouting?'

'Yes darling, but it is okay, mummy will fix it.' She spoke into the top of his head as she held him tightly and started quietly crying into his hair.

After dropping Daniel at school that morning, reassuring him that she really was okay and that she did not need him to stay home to look after her she went home, sat on the sofa and started crying again, big huge sobs her whole body was shaking she wrapped her arms around her legs and rocked back and forth, she must have sat there crying for over an hour as the next time she looked at the clock it was 11am. Annette managed to prise herself from the sofa and attempted the painful walk up the stairs when someone knocked at her front door, she could not see who it was, she was going to ignore it but she thought if it was Simon who had forgotten his keys she would be in trouble, she opened the door with the chain on.

'Delivery' said a voice from the other side of the door.

She released the chain and opened the door wider, the delivery driver handed her the biggest bunch of flowers she had ever seen, she signed for them and shut the door. She reached for the card *I love you* was all it said, she knew they had come from Simon. She took the flowers to the kitchen filled up a vase with water and put them in, she would arrange them later, right now she was exhausted, she dragged her sore, tired body up to Daniel's bedroom, making sure she had her home phone and mobile in her hands, just in case Simon rang to ask about the flowers. Annette then lay down on Daniel's bed and fell into a deep sleep, she stirred as the muffled sound of a house phone rang, still in a sleepy state not realising the noise and assuming she was dreaming she drifted back off to sleep.

Chapter Two

Annette's mother sighed and put the phone down, 'no answer again.' She turned to her husband who was sitting in the armchair opposite her, reading his daily paper.

'Our Annette is so busy we never hear from her, I know she does not like us calling the house but I had to Frank it's been weeks do you think she's okay?'

'I am sure she is fine love,' Frank replied not even putting down his paper.

'I did try her mobile first but the voice kept on telling me, "the number you have dialled is unavailable please try again later.", we should go and visit her Frank, next weekend, we have not seen our daughter or our grandson for ages, what do you think Frank?'

'FRANK!'

'If you want love' Frank sighed and put his paper down. 'You're going to have to wait until we hear from Annette we can't just turn up on the door step,' Frank looked at his wife, her brow creased with worry, 'she will call soon love she always does if not today it will be tomorrow, full of news about meetings, and places her and Daniel have been, she will have an explanation about everything, she always does.'

'It has been so long Frank, Annette and Daniel have not even seen our new place, we have been here over a year, and do you really think she is okay?'

'She has Simon there, it's not like she is on her own.'

'Oh Frank' she sighed, 'what if everything with her and Simon is not as good as what she makes it out to be, I am her mother I should be able to call the house whenever I want to speak to my own daughter and grandson, I don't like that Simon I never have, there's just something about him, why did we ever let her go off with him!'

Call it mother's instinct she just knew all was not as rosy as Annette made it out to be, but she was not sure what to do about it. Frank silently agreed with his wife, not that he would tell her that of course, he hated to see his wife worry although he worried just as much but could not let it show. When they had first met Simon, Frank knew he was no good for his only daughter and would quite happily have told him so, if not for his daughter's feelings. Annette insisted she was happy with him and his daughter's happiness was all that mattered to Frank.

Annette woke with a start, the house was quiet and for a moment she thought it was the middle of night, then she remembered, she picked up her mobile that was now on the floor and checked the time, 'oh my gosh!' she exclaimed to herself it was 2.01pm. Daniel finished school at 3pm and the house was still a mess, she clambered out of Daniel's bed remaking it with care and rushed downstairs. The front room needed hoovering, the sofa cushions needed plumping, the kitchen floor needed mopping, the breakfast things had not been cleared away, the dishwasher was waiting to be unloaded and reloaded; she had done the dishwasher yesterday and the day before but Simon liked it done every day even if it was not full. He was very house proud but did not want to lift a finger in keeping it tidy himself. Annette rushed around for an hour. By the time she had left for the school run at 3.10 the house was done, although now she was late for Daniel but Simon would be happy, or so she hoped. She had taken a couple of extra strong pain killers but her head and body still ached. Thankfully most people had already collected their children and Daniel was the only child left in the playground, she parked the car and rushed in. Daniel was standing by a tree in the playground, she waved to him as he looked up and he smiled at her, she smiled back, no matter how bad Simon treated her, she had to thank him for one thing, he had given her Daniel, he was the most important thing in her life and whatever happened nothing would ever come between them.

Just as Annette reached the tree where Daniel was standing, another mother walked past holding her small child's hand, her face paled as she passed Annette, she whispered to Annette 'you don't have to put up with it you know, there are people that can help you,'

Annette felt her face flush bright red and turned away with embarrassment, she had managed to cover most of the bruising with makeup but she knew she was still a mess.

'Help with what mummy?' Daniel asked.

'What did that lady say you needed help with?'

'Nothing darling she was not talking to me.'

'She was talking to you mum' Daniel frowned.

'No she was not talking to me' Annette replied sternly, now stop going on about it!'

She saw the confused, hurt look on Daniel's face and felt guilty, it was not his fault he was only asking a question, it was that stupid woman's fault for interfering. What did she know about her life anyway!

'How about I cook your favourite for dinner tonight?'

'Can I have toad in the hole?' Daniel replied cheering up, 'with loads of tomato ketchup and can we have chocolate ice cream with sprinkles and sauce for afters too?' he asked on now grinning.

'Of course you can' smiled Annette grabbing hold of his hand stiffly skipping back to the car, Daniel now laughing as she dragged him behind her trying to make him skip along with her too.

She and Daniel had a fun and happy evening together, Daniel had helped to make the dinner, he had made the batter and poured it over the sausages. Daniel even managed to persuade her to let him have five scoops of chocolate ice cream with multi coloured sprinkles, three scoops was the most he was usually allowed.

A few hours later she had just finished tucking Daniel in to his bed, when she heard Simon come in, her heart skipped a beat as she frantically tried to gather a mental picture of downstairs, Annette pictured in her head everything she had done, everything was tidied and put away, the place was spotless, table polished, Simon's dinner was ready in the oven waiting for him just like it was every day, she froze when she heard him call her name, she felt sick with fear as she remembered the flowers, she'd never had time to arrange them before she had left to go school and her and Daniel were having such a great time together she never gave it a second thought. The flowers were still in their cellophane wrapper in the vase on the kitchen window sill, her legs were shaking as she walked down the stairs his coat was hung on the banister and his shoes were neatly lined up in the hallway.

'Yes' she managed to reply trying to keep the panic in her voice under control.

'I was just putting Daniel to bed.'

She had left Daniel listening to his CD in bed with his head phones on.

'What's this?' Simon spat.

As Annette walked into the kitchen, he was holding the flowers in his hands.

'You lazy, good for nothing, ungrateful, fat bitch! 'You couldn't even be bothered to take the flowers out of the wrapping, how hard is that to manage?, even a thick bitch like you should of managed to unwrap the flowers, what have you been doing all fucking day?, sitting on your fat, fucking arse watching daytime TV?'

He walked towards Annette pure hatred in his eyes and she noticed that a vein in his forehead had popped out and was throbbing, he raised his fist, Annette put her arms above her head to try and protect herself, just as he was about to bring his fist down on her,

'Mum! mum!' called Daniel from upstairs.

'Mum! can you help my Cd's not working?'

She looked at Simon and held her breath; he dropped his arm and muttered something she did not totally hear.

'You'll pay for this you ungrateful bitch.' Were the only words she managed to hear.

He turned away from her and walked out the back door, taking the flowers with him, she heard the back gate click open, then click shut, he must have gone to the pub she thought, breathing a sigh of relief she ran upstairs to help Daniel.

Annette opened her eyes she was still on Daniel's bed, he was curled up asleep next to her, she lay there listening to his breathing and felt a warm rush of love run through her body, she must have dozed off again. She awoke when she heard the front door slam, Simon must be home, she heard his footsteps on the way up the stairs they were heavy and she could hear him dragging his body along the wall as he climbed the stairs, steaming drunk she assumed to herself. Her breathing quickened as his footsteps walked along the upstairs hallway, she gripped the covers tight around her, his footsteps stopped as he walked into their bedroom, she heard the click as he turned the bedroom light on and must of realised she was not in their matrimonial bed, his footsteps started up again, she tried to control her breathing as he walked into Daniel's bedroom he paused in the doorway for a second or two. Annette could smell the stale smoke, alcohol and what smelt like a faint whiff of cheap perfume. Annette pretended to be sleeping her heart pounding in her chest, after what felt like hours he finally turned and stumbled his way into their bedroom. Annette let out a relieved sigh, she pulled the covers up to her chin making sure Daniel was still covered put her arm around him and fell back to sleep.

Chapter Three

Annette awoke with a stiff neck and a cold back, Daniel was still asleep next to her with most of the covers wrapped around him, she slowly rolled herself out of Daniel's bed stood up and rubbed her sore neck, she looked at the clock on the wall it was 7.15am. Simon should have left for work hours ago, she must have slept very well as she never heard him leave. She decided to give Daniel another fifteen minutes in bed, that would give her time to have a nice hot shower and hopefully ease her stiff neck, that's what happens when you share a single bed with a six year old she thought. Annette walked into the bathroom she had decided to repaint a light blue, but had not got around to yet, she had also decided to replace the broken mirror with a nice new one, it had a blue mounting to match the colour the walls were going to be. Annette was going to make a start on it this weekend, by the time the house was to Simon's standards she had very limited spare time until it was Daniel's bedtime and she liked to spend as much time with Daniel as she could once she had picked him up from school. Simon would not have been happy seeing paint pots etc left lying around. Simon was going away this weekend for a business conference so her and Daniel could have it done by the time he got back on Sunday night, after she had taken Daniel to school she would stop by the hardware store and buy the paint and mirror she had seen advertised in the magazine, Annette had her shower and called Daniel down for breakfast, she told him they were going to have a busy weekend but it was a surprise, for when daddy comes back from his conference. Daniel was excited as she said good bye to him at the school gates.

'I love it when Dad's away for the weekend mummy we have so much fun and your "happy mummy" again.'

Annette was naïve in a way, she was kidding herself that Daniel did not know what had been going on between her and his father but of course he did, how could he not. Every day when he came home from school he'd notice the house was spotless and as soon as six pm came he could see how tense and nervous his mother became. He knew it was because his father was due home, he also knew if his father's dinner was not hot and ready and waiting for when he walked through the door then his mother would get another punch, his father was careful not to hit his mother in front of him but he saw the bruises and the way she cowered away from his father every time he went near her. He had also heard her crying a lot, she used to lock herself in the bathroom and pretend to be running a bath but he could hear her sometimes, sobbing over the sound of the running water, sometimes she would be halfway through preparing dinner and Daniel would ask if she was okay, Annette would always say 'yes darling I am okay, it's just the onions making my eyes water.' Daniel could see for himself that his mum did not cook with onions every time.

He wished he was older and could hit his father back, to make him hurt the way he hurt his mother, he wanted to be able to hit his father so hard that he would be scared of him and would never hurt his mother again.

Annette had gone to the hardware store after dropping Daniel at school and had found the paint and mirror, she had also stopped at the supermarket and bought blue toilet roll to match, she could not wait until Daniel came home. Annette returned home and unpacked what she had bought, blue paint, two rollers, two trays, the blue mirror and the matching toilet roll. She had noticed a few people staring at her, the bruising had gone down a bit but was still faintly visible, she had big circles under her eyes and it must have looked like she was carrying the weight of the world on her shoulders, she looked at what she had bought with a smile and then walked into the front room. Annette picked up the phone and called her mother who she knew had been worried about her, her mother had wanted to come up and visit that weekend. Annette told her that, herself, Daniel and Simon were fine; she told her how Simon had been working really hard and about the wonderful bunch of flowers he had delivered to her "Just because he loves me" she quoted. Annette explained how this weekend was a bad weekend as she and Daniel were redecorating the bathroom as a surprise for Simon when he came home.

Her mother thought Annette sounded down and tired but did not want to say anything in case she upset her. Annette's mother hated the fact they lived so far away and even though her father would not admit it to anyone, he was dearly missing both his daughter and grandson, he had his suspicions that something was wrong, although he thought Annette would tell him what it was if and when she was ready. She sounded so excited about redecorating the bathroom he did not want to spoil the tone of the conversation.

Annette and Daniel had a great weekend and when Simon came home Daniel proudly showed him the bathroom, it was just as Annette had wanted it and it really had been a good weekend, the walls were pale blue and the mirror matched perfectly, Simon had even smiled when Daniel had shown him the matching blue toilet roll, but behind Daniel's back he gave Annette a really horrible look and she quickly went downstairs to serve the dinner.

A couple of month's had passed, it was now just two days away from Daniel's seventh birthday, they were taking him to the zoo for his birthday as they had planned.

'Just two more days to go' she had told Daniel when he'd asked her yet again when they were going.

'One day to go' she told him when she dropped him off at school on the Friday, she went home and was cleaning the house ready for when Simon came home, she did not want to do any housework the next day as that was Daniel's day and she was not planning to be in for most of it, she was half way through the housework when the house phone rang she picked it up.

'Hello' Annette said when she answered the phone.

There was silence at the other end.

'Hello is anyone there?' Annette asked.

Annette heard a click, whoever was at the end of the phone had put it down without saying anything, must have been a wrong number she thought to herself as she carried on with the housework, the house was done by the time she had got Daniel from school. She had finally got an excited Daniel to sleep when Simon had rung to say he was working late.

Simon arrived home from work that night, she smelt the same cheap perfume on him again, enough is enough she thought to herself and waited until he was asleep, thankfully this did not take him long because of the amount he must have drunk, he was flat on his back snoring loudly. Slowly she crept out of bed and felt around for Simon's trousers they were slung on the floor like they were every night, she felt around his trouser pockets and found the phone. With trembling hands she pulled the phone out of his pocket, she stood in the dark with Simon's phone in her hand wondering if it was the right thing to do or not, her heart was pounding in her chest as she looked over at Simon. He was snoring, still asleep, right or wrong she had to know if anything was going on, thank goodness he was still sleeping, she took a deep breath and looked at the screen on his phone. She scrolled through the menu options until she had found what she was looking for, "Text message inbox", the first text she saw was from someone called "John Smith" she held her breath as she pressed view to read it.

Where are you? The first text from "John" read.

You had best not be at home !!!!!.

The texts from "John" continued.

I just rang your house and your bitch of a wife answered!!.

Oh so now you bother to reply!! Followed the next text.

Annette read on, not really wanting to know anymore but could not stop herself as she continued through his texts, she was feeling sick as she read the next one and felt the bile rising in her throat.

Don't worry I never told her about us, I may change my mind! You have an hour before I call again and tell her everything.

Annette took a sharp intake of breath at reading the last one, she realised Simon had stopped snoring, she quickly glanced at Simon and froze to the spot, he was awake and staring right at her.

Annette dropped the phone in shock.

'Wot da FUCK you thinxsh youarrre doing' Simon slurred.

'I, I' Annette stammered, panic rising in her body and her heart starting to pound hard in her chest.

'I said wot da FUCK you thinxsh youarrre doing.'

Simon got out of bed and stumbled towards Annette; she bent down and grabbed the phone, her arm outstretched towards the floor. She tried to hand him the phone when he grabbed her by the hand.

'I...I...thought I heard it ring' she offered him as a way of an explanation.

He held her hand and was twisting her wrist.

'You're hurting me' she said.

Simon twisted her wrist harder.

'Please don't hurt me please' she began to beg.

He twisted her hand again and again as Annette dropped the phone to the floor, 'please stop, please' Annette begged, tears of pain now flowing down her face.

'You nosey little bitch' he spat in her face.

'What did you see?'

'Nothing...nothing...I thought it rang, I did not see anything, I thought it rang, please don't hurt me, please don't, please' she begged him.

Annette screamed as he twisted her hand so fast that she fell on the floor clutching her arm in agony.

'Oh my God my arm' she sobbed the pain was so intense.

'That's what you get for fucking snooping you...'

The end of his sentence was cut off as their bedroom door flew open.

'Mum' Daniel shouted as he rushed to his mum's side.

'Your stupid mother tripped over the end of the bed and hurt her arm, go back to bed' Simon told Daniel sharply.

'I need to go to hospital' Annette said quietly, she was shaking with shock and fear as the pain throbbed through her arm, she could see the swelling and bruising starting to appear, crying in pain she cradled her arm.

'We need to call a cab' she managed to stammer out.

They got back from the hospital three hours later, Annette's wrist was broken and one of the bones in her arm was fractured, the doctor looked at her with sadness in his eyes as she explained how she had got out of bed for a glass of water and had tripped over her slippers which were at the end of the bed, she tried to laugh and make a joke about how accident prone she was, Simon said nothing.

Annette was due back at hospital in a few hours time to have a more permanent plaster cast, Daniel's zoo trip was now cancelled, Daniel had said he understood but Annette had heard him crying in his bedroom, Simon had still said nothing.

After Annette had got her permanent cast fitted "for four weeks" the doctor had told her, Simon said he had received a phone call, he needed to go into work as something urgent had come up which could not wait until Monday. Annette was sure she had never heard his phone ring, so after a cab had dropped Annette and Daniel home, Simon went to work. Annette and Daniel opened his birthday presents, they had bought him an xbox and two games. Daniel was so excited he went up to his room and set the console up. Annette's parents had sent two jumpers and a voucher for a games shop so he could pick another game when he wanted. Maddie had sent him a brand new bike, she always spoilt Daniel every birthday and every Christmas, Daniel was the closest thing to having a child of her own and she spoiled him rotten.

Annette was twinged with sadness and was feeling so guilty, Daniel had been so looking forward to the zoo, she wished that Simon had let her parents visit so Daniel could say thank you in person and not over the phone like he had done for so many years, what was happening to her life she wondered, was this as bad as it got, she shuddered as Simon's words echoed around her head "If you ever try to leave me I will kill you." She still did not doubt this for a second, she went upstairs to sit with Daniel while he played on his games, and she told him again how sorry she was about him missing his zoo trip.

'Never mind Mum accidents happen, we can always go in a few weeks when your arms better or perhaps Dad will take us next weekend.'

'We will see' she replied to Daniel. Although I doubt it very much she thought sadly to herself.

Simon came home when Daniel was already in bed, he had wanted to see his Dad to say thank you for his xbox, she had let Daniel stay up until 10pm but still no sign of Simon, Annette explained daddy was very busy at work but he would be very sorry he missed his birthday, so reluctantly Daniel finally went to bed. Annette was in bed trying to find a comfortable position to lie in, which was not easy having a rock hard cast on your arm.

Simon walked in and looked at her, 'Mind your slippers tonight' was all he said as he got into bed beside her, he turned his back on her and went to sleep.

Annette laid on her back staring at the ceiling, he did not even ask about Daniel she thought, as a cascade of fresh hot tears streamed silently down her cheeks and dripped on to the pillow under her head.

Annette's cast had been taken off finally after five weeks, the broken wrist and fractured arm had healed perfectly the doctor had said while looking at the repeated x-rays. Annette's parents had finally got hold of her and had planned to visit in a few weekends time. They were going to make it a week-long visit and had booked a hotel for half way through the journey; they were leaving their home Friday evening for the first four hour haul and then continuing the journey after lunch on the Saturday.

Things were not going very well for Annette and Daniel, Daniel had come home with no school jumper and his pens were going missing day by day. The day before her parents arrived, Annette received a phone call from the school just after lunch and was asked to come to the office straight away to see the head teacher.

When Annette got there Daniel's eyes were red and swollen from crying and his jumper was torn, 'Daniel what on earth has happened?'

'I think you had better sit down' said the head teacher while offering Annette a chair.

Annette listened in shock and looked down at the floor in shame, the head teacher explained that some of the older children had been calling Daniel names and were bullying him and there were rumours circulating in the playground regarding his father and a local barmaid.

'Mum' Daniel sobbed 'they also said my dad was a "wife beater" and I will turn out just like him unless they beat it out of me, that's what they were trying to do to me mum, beat it out of me, what's going on mummy has daddy done something wrong?'

Tears welled up in Annette's eyes as she looked at her poor Son, the head teacher said Daniel could go home early as it was a Friday and he was only going to miss the last hour of school, as they stood up to leave the head teacher put her arm on Annette's shoulder and pressed a leaflet into her hands 'there are people who can help' she quietly told Annette.

"We are here to help" the leaflet stated "Domestic abuse helpline".

On the way home Daniel was asking a lot of questions Annette hated lying to him but really did not want him knowing the truth either.

She changed the subject by reminding Daniel his grandparents were coming up to see him tomorrow afternoon and how great it would be. Annette had managed to put them off for over a year and felt guilty, this time she was going to finally see them, she had missed them so much and was really looking forward to it she crossed her fingers and hoped Simon would be sober or better still called away to work for the whole weekend.

After putting Daniel to bed that night Annette locked herself in the bathroom and cried, she knew she had to do something, she knew she had to get away, she was scared, very scared! Simon had said he would never let her go, but she knew she had to get away, far away just her and Daniel, far away from here, far away from Simon and the horrible kids at Daniel's school. Annette guessed it must have been the mother she had seen at school not that long ago the one who had told her the same as the head teacher had done, why people couldn't just have minded their own business and left her and Daniel alone. Annette reached into her handbag and pulled out the leaflet she had been given "Domestic Abuse Helpline" it was a 24 hour 0800 number so it was free to call and would not show up on their phone bill if she called, it also said they provided places where women and children could stay safely. She decided she would call them after her parents had gone, her parents did not need to be involved in this, no one else needed to be involved she told herself silently, Annette knew she needed help if not for her then she would do it for Daniel.

It was 4.00pm. Her parents would be arriving soon they had left the hotel just after lunch which was four hours away. Her black eye from last week was almost gone and the makeup she had applied ever so carefully had disguised the rest. Over the last few years she had worked out how to use the make up to hide the bruises and cuts Simon had inflicted on her so very well. She used concealer first thickly, a thin covering of foundation, followed by another touch up of concealer and then finished off with a brush over of bronzing pearls which made her look glowing and fresh. She looked around the house it was as spotless as ever and she had bought a couple of bunches of flowers, one now in the hallway and the other on the front room coffee table, the only room that was still a mess was the kitchen. Simon was still not back she had reminded him this morning her parents were coming and he announced he had a meeting to attend that would probably take all day and he was going to the pub for a quick drink after, but would not be late, she and Daniel had baked chocolate cookies and fresh bread for her parents arrival, they were just tidying this up when Annette heard the familiar scrape of a door key trying to find its way into the lock on the front door, 'go and listen to your Walkman' she quickly said to Daniel, knowing full well that Simon was drunk and she hoped he would just come in and sleep it off, she really did not want her parents to see the state of Simon and even more she did not want Daniel to see his father like this, as much as she now loathed Simon there was no need for Daniel to witness his father's drunken behaviour. Annette did not want it to be here and now the real reasons for mummy being so clumsy coming to light. Daniel tried to protest but something in the way his mum said, 'quickly upstairs now, listen to your music as loud as you want,' made him scarper off up the stairs just as Simon managed to put the key in to the lock. Annette quickly looked around at the kitchen, there was still a bit of flour on the side, the cookies and the bread were cooling on the side next to the sink, she turned around shaking and braced herself for Simon's entrance. As she had rightly guessed Simon was steaming drunk and came towards her into the kitchen, at the kitchen door he looked around and took in the mess, he lunged towards her and before she even had a chance to react he had punched her in the mouth, she fell back into the sideboard and knocked the cookies and bread into the bubbly sink of washing up she had frantically been trying to clean, Annette tasted blood in her mouth and realised he must have split her lip open, he was drunkenly shouting at her about the mess and what a bad wife and mother she was when Daniel appeared in the doorway, 'Dad what are you doing?,'

'ello son' came Simon's slurred reply 'I'm elping your muver tidy up in time for your wonderful grandparent's visit.'

Simon looked at his now bleeding, sobbing wife who was trying to fish out the cookies from the soapy washing up water,

'Mum are you all right?' came a small voice from behind her, 'what's happened to the cookies?' Annette tried to hide her face, tears now streaming freely down her face, partly from the pain of her lip, but more so for Daniel having to see what was going on and seeing the now soggy cookies floating about in the sink.

'Mum look at me,' pleaded Daniel

'Your muver's a bitch' spat out Simon, 'She threw the cookies in the water and said you had burnt them.' Annette looked at Simon and saw the vicious look in his eyes, she was scared for herself but more for Daniel right now.

'What happened to your lip mummy?'

'She got what was coming to her' slurred Simon

Daniel's face went pale and he slowly said 'Did you do that to mummy?' pointing to her lip,

Just like all the other times Annette replied 'I just hurt myself being clumsy', she was trying to protect Daniel from the raw truth.

'So what if I did' butted in Simon, 'what you gonna to do about it, you little fucking shit?' Daniel went to hit his father, with his fist drawn back he lunged at his father Annette quickly grabbed Daniel back and pulled him behind her she shouted at Simon,

'Leave us alone, NOW!'

'Yes leave us alone' Daniel echoed in a small but stern voice. Simon looked at them both, Daniel now standing silently behind his mother; Simon shrugged his shoulders at them both and staggered out the back door, Annette closed and locked the back door behind him before sinking onto the floor with Daniel in her arms both of them crying.

Annette heard a car pull up outside, 'Quick Daniel' she said getting to her feet 'Quick outside, nanny and granddad are here!' She took Daniel's hand and together they ran out of the house, she grabbed her handbag from the banister on the way past the stairs, not even caring if the front door had shut behind them, 'Get in the car' she told Daniel 'Quick' as she opened the back door to her parent's car, 'Drive dad' she told him as she shut and locked the car door behind them both. Frank looked at his daughter in his rear view mirror, He took in the red swollen eyes she had from crying and then he saw the swollen cut lip, 'Don't worry my darling' he said putting the car swiftly into drive, 'We're going home' and with that he sped off. Annette was clutching Daniel tightly to her he was still crying. 'Sorry Mum' Annette croaked, 'shush my love' her mother soothed 'no need for sorry, you're both safe now.' Josie looked at her husband with tears in her eyes, he reached over with one hand and patted his wife on her knee 'they *are* safe now' he softly said to her, 'Safe.'

Chapter Four

Annette had been living with her parents for over a year, she and Daniel shared the spare room, Daniel was almost nine years old now. Daniel had the main bed and Annette had a blow up bed on the floor it was not much but she was happy. Simon had telephoned her constantly; she ignored his calls, in the end she had to get a new mobile number as he was calling her up to forty times a day leaving all sorts of horrible threatening messages. Annette's parents had urged her many a time to go to the police but Annette did not want to, she was just relieved to be far away from him. Thank goodness she had never managed to persuade Simon to go and visit her parents new home, she had told him they had moved but he never asked where so she had never told him, the only place she had written down her parents new phone number and address was in her address book which she carried around in her handbag with her, at least she had grabbed that on the way out of the door. Her parents never asked any questions but gradually Annette let the whole last few years of her life come to light and her parents sat and listened while she cried telling them about the barmaid and the other times we already know about, she never told them the full details that was something she never wanted to share.

Her mother said that Annette should have told them but Annette explained how she never wanted them involved and thought he would change back to the kind loving Simon she had first met, her parents understood; well she thought they did as they never asked about any of it again.

Daniel started his new school and quickly made friends, if anyone asked about his Scottish accent he just said we used to live in Scotland until mummy and daddy did not love each other anymore, and then we moved in with nanny and granddad. Daniel had told Annette he still loved his daddy and asked if that was okay, although he did not want to see his daddy again as he had made him very scared, he went on to tell Annette that sometimes he had heard her crying, and he heard daddy shouting at her and calling her bad names, Annette was even more sure she had done the right thing after hearing that, she was very happy they were both getting their lives life back on track.

Maddie came around most days after she had finished work, Maddie owned a small but expensive boutique, many of the outfits she had designed herself, while Annette was doing her interior design course's Maddie was doing a fashion design course, which was the perfect job for Maddie and a good thing considering the amount of clothes Maddie actually owned and bought. Annette had been looking for a job for the last couple of months, it had taken her around seven months to properly get her head around the fact she had actually left Simon. At first she felt guilty, wondering how Simon would cope on his own, doing his own cooking, working the washing machine, then she remembered how he treated her and the guilt subsided, she was now strong enough to start looking for a job. Her parents were not well off; they only had a small amount of savings from the sale of the old house and their pensions. She felt she could no longer impose on them and had to get a job, so she and Daniel could have a house of their own soon, that's why Maddie had turned up today. She had taken the day off work and had brought a lot of clothes with her, Annette had been walking a lot due to the fact she had left her car on the driveway when she left and had no intention of going back to get the car or anything else for that matter, she had taken with her everything she needed, herself and Daniel. Daniel was upset when he realised he had to leave his things behind but slowly with help from Maddie and Annette's parents all the things Daniel had left behind had been replaced, some of the things were better than what he'd had in the first place. Maddie showed Annette some of the clothes she had bought with her, Annette laughed and said I would never fit into them, Maddie replied don't be silly they are all your size, just a few things I had at the back of my wardrobe for when I had put on a bit of weight, Annette knew this was not true Annette was still a size 12 and

Maddie had always been a size 10, no matter what Maddie consumed she never put on any weight. She hugged her best friend and insisted she would pay her back, Maddie would not have any of it insisting they really were from the back of her wardrobe and there was no need for any payment, (the wardrobe, meaning the back of the stock cupboard at work and that they were gifts), 'Now let's get you ready', 'How are you feeling?' Annette was nervous; she had never been to a job interview before and was worrying about every small detail. Annette had been flicking through the free weekly paper when a large advert had caught her eye.

The Job

We are looking for an enthusiastic full time Receptionist to join our prestigious Property development company, Monday to Friday 9.30am till 5.00pm

The Role

The role involves answering incoming calls; distributing incoming post; meeting and greeting visitors and ensuring the reception area is kept tidy

The Company

The Company is family run and offers a friendly working environment, and free parking

The Person

We are looking for an enthusiastic candidate, previous reception experience not needed as training can be provided. You will need to have a pleasant telephone manner, good communication skills, be willing to learn and be of smart appearance

To Apply

Please send CV in writing to Carrington's 115 High Street

Why not Annette thought as she wrote her CV and posted it off, she worked a couple of days a week for Maddie in the shop and the occasional Saturday which brought in some money so she could save a bit and give her parents some, although she wanted a proper job of her own and not one that she felt had been given to her out of pity, even though Maddie assured her it had not, she loved working with Maddie and enjoyed every day, but she also knew that there was no need for her. Maddie and Julie, the sales assistant, had been fine working the shop as the two of them had done without a third person since the shop had opened five years ago. Annette had forgotten all about applying for the job with Carrington's until a letter arrived addressed to her, she gasped as she read the letter she had been shortlisted for an interview which is why Maddie was now with her and they were going through the clothes trying to find something smart. They both chose a smart black trouser suit and Annette wore a pink fitted shirt underneath the jacket, she tied her hair up in a ponytail to finish off her smart but professional look. It was almost time to go, Annette's hands were shaking and she had not even left the house yet, a quick cup of tea with two large sugars Maddie instructed and dragged her downstairs, 'oh my goodness' her mother exclaimed as Annette and Maddie walked down the stairs 'don't you look smart, you could pass for the boss couldn't she Frank, FRANK!' 'Yes love' said Frank, he looked up and saw his daughter, she looked really happy but nervous, her eyes were bright and sparkled, and the suit looked perfect on her, 'good luck my love' he said to Annette, 'I'm sure you will get this job they would be mad not to offer it to you on the spot.'

Annette smiled, she hoped her father was right she really wanted this job and despite her nerves she felt happy and walked to Maddie's car with a big grin on her face and her handbag slung over her shoulder. The drive to the offices of the property developers was not a long one, Annette checked her make up in the vanity mirror and took a few deep breaths to steady her nerves, Maddie looked over at her and smiled, 'You really look good you know, your dad's right they would be mad not to offer you the job.'

Annette and Maddie grinned at each other as they pulled into a parking space in the office car park,

'Shit!, Shit!, Shit!' exclaimed Annette to Maddie 'it's really happening what if I say something wrong or end up in a coughing fit or need a wee or something?'

Maddie leaned over and hugged Annette you will be fine, she reached behind her seat and pulled out a bottle of water and a small box,

'It's for good luck.'

Annette opened the box and inside was a gold charm bracelet,

'Oh Maddie it is gorgeous, thank you, you shouldn't have,'

'Yer, yer whatever' replied Maddie and clasped the bracelet around Annette's wrist.

'Now go get yourself that job girl.'

As Annette got out the car she looked back at Maddie, who was grinning like a Cheshire cat,

'I will stay right here waiting for you,'

'Okay' said Annette and took another couple of deep breaths as she walked into the office.

The office was huge and had a nice big reception/waiting area, the desk was in a semi-circle in front of the doors in the middle of the vast space, behind the desk sat a woman who looked in her early twenties or younger, they are never going to hire me thought Annette I'm way too old, she took a small swig of water from the bottle Maddie had given her in the car and with her head up and back straight she walked confidently up to the woman behind the desk to say she was here and ready for her interview.

Her stomach was full of butterflies and she felt like she was going to be sick with nerves, she recalled the same feeling back at school whilst playing the part of a star in the nativity play when she was five years old, she had been sick just before going on stage thankfully into the plastic bag her teacher had given her, Maddie was on stage playing the part of Mary and gave Annette a huge grin, just like the one Maddie had given her forty five minutes ago as Annette had got out the car. After the young Maddie had grinned

Annette knew she would be the best star the parents and teachers had ever seen and she was, her parents, her teacher and Maddie had all told her so after the play had finished.

Thankfully Annette was not sick and did not need a wee on this occasion, nothing had gone wrong when an hour later Annette rushed back to Maddie's car, still where it was parked in exactly the same place, just like Maddie had said it would be she opened the door and got in.

'Well' said Maddie when Annette had got in and closed the door,

'I don't know' said Annette 'they said they would let me know when they had finished interviewing everyone else on Friday.'

Today was Tuesday so it was going to be a long week. Annette tried to keep herself busy but found herself jumping every time the phone rang, more often than not it was Maddie calling during her lunch break from the shop asking if Annette had heard anything yet, the phone rang on Friday afternoon and as she had been all week Annette jumped and ran down the stairs two at a time, shouting to her parents she would answer it, her parents were sitting in her front room as Annette ran past them to grab the phone.

'Hello' said Annette politely into the phone,

'Good afternoon,' came a posh voice from the other end of the phone, 'I am calling from Carrington's, would it be possible to speak with Ms Annette Johnson please?'

'Speaking' come Annette's nervous reply,

'I see' said Annette a few minutes later,

'Thank you for letting me know,'

'Goodbye.'

As Annette put the phone back in its cradle she turned towards her parents, she knew they had been trying not to listen, but she also knew they had heard every word.

'Never mind love' said her mother as she looked at Annette's glum face trying to hide the disappointment in her voice.

'I'm sure something else will come along soon.'

Her father looked at her and smiled 'So' he said slowly,

'So' said Annette equally slowly,

'I got the job' she suddenly burst out unable to keep the excitement in and hide the grin off her face a moment longer.

'Pardon' said her mother as her father jumped up to give her a hug.

'I got the job mum; they want me to start in two weeks' she said as the tears of joy trickled down her face.

'Oh love I am so happy for you' her mother stood up and joined in the hug, 'Daniel's going to be over the moon,' she said.

Annette saw her parents exchange a strange look as they smiled at each other, what are they up too thought Annette.

Maddie screamed excitedly down the phone when Annette called to tell her the news and when she told Daniel he said 'I knew you could do it mum, I knew you could,' hugging her tightly around her waist.

Everything about her parents behaviour became clear the next morning when Annette awoke to find the house empty and a note stating her parents and Daniel had gone shopping and they would be a couple of hours, they had bought her some chocolate muffins and croissants for breakfast which were in the bread bin as a congratulations on getting the job, that was odd thought Annette as she put the croissants in the oven, today was Wednesday her parents did their shopping on Mondays come rain or shine, the shops were normally quieter then and her father could not stand busy shops full of people. While she was eating her now warm croissants she tried to call Maddie, no reply at work or home which was odd as Maddie was normally nowhere else in the mornings, Annette also tried her mobile which was switched off, Maddie never had her mobile switched off!

Her parents and Daniel arrived home a couple of hours later, Daniel was in first, he burst in through the front door like a hurricane; Daniel grabbed hold of his mum's hand and dragged her outside, where to her surprise stood her parents and Maddie. 'What's going on?' said Annette as she took in the people around her all grinning like Cheshire cats, 'take these' said Daniel pushing something into Annette's hand, she looked down; a set of car keys attached to a key ring "Annette's keys" was the first thing Annette noticed the key ring read, 'what the?' said Annette as her son pushed her towards a light blue Nissan Micra which was parked outside her parents' home. 'Look inside mum another surprise,'

Annette looked inside the car and there, another set of keys sat, on top of a map, a map that had a big red X drawn in the middle of it. Annette could not take it all in she started shaking as she looked around at the four beaming faces and slowly understood what was going on, 'Come on mum get in' said Daniel as he opened the passenger door and got in,

'It's from all of us' said her father at last, 'we could not have you getting the bus to work every day now could we.'

'You bought this for me' stammered Annette, 'me?' 'This is my car, for me, mine, my car?'

'YES' they all said at once.

'I picked the colour mum' said Daniel from inside the car.

Annette stood there on the pavement in shock as she watched her mum close the front door and double lock it, 'Come on mum we have a treasure map to follow' said Daniel.

Maddie and her parents got in to the back of the car, 'Where are we going?' Annette asked as she got in the car and started the engine. 'Just follow the map mum!' said Daniel impatiently. So that's just what they did.

The map lead them just a few roads away from where they had started and as Annette pulled into a driveway of a house she had never seen before, 'What's going on?' she started to say as everyone was getting out the car, 'Don't forget the keys' Daniel instructed her, she grabbed the keys from the dash where Daniel had put them while he had done the map reading, 'What's going on?' asked Annette again as she walked up to the door where everyone else was already waiting, 'Open the door mum, open the door' said Daniel excitedly beside her, as Annette unlocked the front door. 'Welcome to your new home' said her mother, 'if you like it that is, we arranged a viewing for you and the landlord said you can move in right away'.

'My what?' Annette stammered staring at both her mother and father.

'You heard' laughed Maddie,

'My home?' replied Annette,

'Yes yours and Daniel's.'

'But how, when, why?'

'I hope you don't mind' her mother started to explain; 'Daniel saw the house vacant for rent in the paper a few days ago and he said that's the kind of house you wanted, so we rang the number and it turns out the landlord is a friend of mine and your father's, he let us have the keys to show you around, he even knocked a few pounds off the rental price for you.'

New car and now the house it was all Annette could take as she stumbled into the house.

As she walked around the house, with Daniel dragging her into every room she was still in shock, she wondered if it was a dream and she would wake up in her bed at her parent's home with Daniel snoring beside her. It was not a dream it was real, it really was her house and her new car was parked out front. Unbeknown to Annette her parents actually had quite a bit of money left over from the sale of their house and from saving over years, they had enough to give Annette the deposit and first month's rent, as much as they loved having her and Daniel to stay, a place of their own was just what they needed. It turned out Daniel had known about everything and had even seen the house before, when her parents had arranged the first viewing, they had taken Daniel with them, the house was perfect for Annette and Daniel, two bedrooms a cosy front room, a large kitchen and even the garden was fine, the house was perfect for them, just as her parents knew it would be.

The rest of the week and a half was a flurry of activity as they moved what they had accumulated at her parent's house in to their own home, Annette and Daniel had chosen and bought new beds, a double for Annette's room and a single for Daniel's. Most other things they needed had been donated from her parents and Maddie's own homes, a few items like the wardrobes and the kitchen table with odd chairs had been bought from a second hand furniture shop in town, the sofa was her parents old one, as too were the coffee table and two sets of drawers that were now in Annette's bedroom. They had put these things in storage when they had sold their old house as they had a feeling they might come in handy one day.

Annette and Daniel had bought a matching kettle and toaster set that was on sale in a well known department store and had picked up matching tea, coffee, sugar and bread bin to match in a nice yellow, Annette had decided when she had a spare moment she was going to paint the kitchen a bright yellow colour to match. Before Annette knew it, the days had flown by and it was now the second Friday in her new home, as she sat in her own front room, Maddie called to say that herself and Annette were going out that night to celebrate, her parents had agreed to babysit and would be round at 6pm so she had time to get herself ready.

Chapter Five

Annette was happy with her life just the way it was, just her and Daniel in their nice cosy two bed house, she still had her parents living just down the road from her and saw them often.

Her parents adored Daniel, they had bonded well during the months Annette has stayed with them and they never minded babysitting for Annette.

They did wish sometimes Annette would ask them more often to have Daniel so she could go out, after everything she had been through she more than deserved to let her hair down once in a while.

She left Daniel with a kiss and handed her mother a long list of instructions detailing what time his bedtime was, how he liked to be read a story, what kind of story, warm milk for bed but just half a mug, her parents already knew this and more but they did not mind the list, they knew how she hated leaving Daniel in the evenings even though it was just for a few hours.

Finally off she went with Maddie who had already made Annette go back into the house and change her top, Annette was originally wearing a not very flattering black top and black trousers. Maddie knew this would be Annette's outfit of choice for the evening so she had also brought along one of her "own" (so she said but we won't go through all that again). The top was silver and backless which went very well with Annette's black trousers. Maddie then had to practically drag Annette out of her house down the front path and into the waiting cab.

Maddie also knew how much Annette hated leaving Daniel but she understood after everything that had happened. Daniel was her whole life.

Maddie also knew it would do Annette the world of good to get out for a few hours and have a giggle together.

It was an exclusive club, well worth going to, Maddie had pulled quite a lot of strings to get them both on the guest list for tonight, who knows they may even spot a famous footballer or two.

Chapter Six

He had been watching her for most of the evening, she looked happy and was dancing away with her friend. she was unaware that a few metres away he was watching her, mesmerised by how her long dark wavy hair shone in the flashing lights and how her black trousers and silver backless top really showed off her trim figure, he felt an overwhelming urge to march right over to her and sweep her up into his arms and declare himself, hers forever!

His closest and oldest male friend Nathan was watching him and followed his eyes to where he was staring, he was staring at her, she threw her head back and laughed at something one of her friends had said, the blonde one; Nathan had noticed she was in a tight pink top and little Denim skirt with legs that seemed to go on forever, she was the one who had made the girl in the black trousers laugh.

Nathan had to turn away from the girl in pink as he felt the familiar stirring in his loins and had to shake it off, he was due to get married to his long term girlfriend in three month's time, Kathleen the daughter of one of his mother's oldest and dearest friends a year younger than himself, they used to play together in the playpen and share baths together when they were little so it was no surprise when they got together and stayed together, with the wedding not far away they were very happy and deeply in love with each other.

As Nathan looked back at the dancing girls he was wondering why James was looking at the black trousered girl. The blonde was much more James's type. The type he just used for sex, it made Nathan laugh that him and James had been best friends for so long, yet have totally the opposite taste in women.

The last of James's conquests as an example was 5' 8", slim, blonde, followed him around like a puppy for the whole nine weeks the relationship lasted, she did everything for him, cooked, cleaned, everything (nine weeks was almost a year in James's terms), eventually he just ignored her calls and eventually sent her a text, saying he had grown out of her and found her too needy and whatever she thought they had together was over!

That was James's style, love em and leave em!

Nathan often wondered if it was Karen's fault James was the way he was now, Karen was James's first love, they met on the first day of high school when they were both eleven and stayed together until Karen turned to James on the last day of school when they were both sixteen and said it's over, I don't love you anymore and I have not done for a while, I am in love with Paul from 6th form and just like that Karen was gone, walked off arm in arm with Paul who was waiting outside. By the time James had digested what she had actually said Karen and Paul had both driven off in Paul's clapped out Ford Fiesta. Nathan did not think James had ever heard from her again.

Annette and Maddie had been at Zeke night club for a couple of hours now, the cab had taken almost fifty min's to get them there but it was well worth the cab fare there and back as it was a great and fairly cheap night out thanks to them being on the guest list which meant free entry and a complimentary bottle of champagne.

Annette felt a hand on her shoulder she tensed up and almost screamed, for one horrible moment the thought it was Simon who had finally tracked her down.

She turned around shaking and saw a pair of very sparkling green eyes looking right in to hers: 'Sorry' she stammered you gave me a fright!'

'Oh gosh,' 'No I'm the one who is sorry it is never my intention to frighten stunningly beautiful women.'

Out of the corner of her eye Annette saw Maddie pretending to stick her fingers down her throat making gagging faces.

'Do I know you?' She enquired to the green eyed man who was very good looking from what she could tell, it was not that dark in the club but the lights were dim. He had blonde messy hair and from what she could see in the dim club lights a nicely defined body (not that she was looking of course).

'In answer to your question (he shouted over the music) no we have never met and really, I don't normally do this, I was going to ask you for your number then I thought you may say no or give me a false one so I wanted to give you my number then it's up to you if you call or not.'

He handed her a business card she looked down at it *James Harrington* he looked at her slightly embarrassed.

It was true he had never given his number to any woman before; they normally throw themselves at him, one woman he met had even written her number on his white shirt in bright pink lipstick, he had to throw that shirt away but he did find out lipstick stains are a pain in the backside to get out of clothes even if your laundry does get taken away twice a week and brought back the same day clean folded and ironed. Throwing that lipstick stained shirt away also saved him the embarrassment of the laundry woman asking if he was sure he did not need the number, she had asked quite a few times before after finding bits of paper with women's numbers scribbled on them normally accompanied by names like Electra, Sexy Lexi, once there was even a Bambi!

James looked at her she really was stunning and had just a hint of make up on her beautiful face 'Sorry' he finally managed to stammer out he realised she was staring at him like he was some kind of nutter.

'I really hope you call.' He finally said to Annette, 'I best go back to my friends; I sincerely hope you enjoy the rest of your evening.'

He turned away and walked back in to crowd, leaving Annette stunned and standing still.

'Well?' said Maddie, once he had gone.

Annette looked again at the card in her hand *James Harrington* it said his name was, Annette shook her head but smiled. 'Well he had some guts I suppose' she said to Maddie,

'He was well fit! If you're not going call him, can I?' Maddie quipped.

Annette laughed at Maddie and put the card in her purse, she was going to throw it away when she got home, she was not interested in men and was not going to be for a long time, even if they were very good looking with stunning green eyes.

By the time James had made it back across the dance floor to Nathan, Nathan was almost rolling around on the floor laughing, tears rolling down his face.

'You should have seen yourself! It was too funny for words, you made a right prat out of yourself mate! you should have gone for the blonde she looked like she was well gagging for it.'

'Piss off!' replied James, he was not laughing or finding Nathan at all funny, in fact he was a bit shocked at what he had just done, his heart was still pounding and his hands damp with sweat, was this the effect that girl had on him or was it just because the nightclub was packed full of hot sweaty bodies?

'Oh well' he sighed to himself 'nothing ventured nothing gained!'

Nathan nudged him as a group of young blonde, giggling, stick thin model types wiggled over to where him and James were standing, a girl in a tight short red dress gave James a flutter of her eye lashes and started to grind her body against his, he was not actually interested his mind was still thinking about whether the stunning brunette would actually call him or not, he really hoped she would.

Nathan whistled and moved on over to one of her friends who was just as model looking as the one James was grinding with.

Maddie and Annette decided to call it a night, they said goodbye to the rest of their friends and walked to the exit, as they were leaving they heard a screeching laugh they both looked over to where a group of stunning looking girls were dancing rather crudely with a couple of guys they could not really see what the guys looked like as the girls were in the way.

Maddie and Annette looked at each other and laughed, someone really should of told the girl in the short red dress that you could see her knickers but she probably already knew that herself. Annette woke up early on Saturday morning, she had arrived home just after 1am, her mother had left as soon as Annette had got in, Daniel was still asleep, she noticed the TV was not on, she looked at the clock it was 4am no wonder he was still asleep.

She tried to get back to sleep but after tossing and turning for a bit and counting sheep nothing would work, she gave up at 4.45am and went downstairs for a glass of water and a pain killer or two.

She had, had a good night out but was now feeling slightly hung over she had only drunk a few vodka and cokes or perhaps they were double shots of vodka, she normally did not drink but her throbbing head and dry mouth was enough of a reminder as to why she chose not to drink.

She ran the tap and filled a glass of cold water and sat down at her kitchen table.

It was a nice kitchen table, she and Daniel had chosen it together yesterday, it was chrome and glass and the chairs had padded seats so they were quite comfortable, the kitchen was one of the places she liked to sit in most of the time, the walls were a bright yellow not a horrible shade it was a nice and bright welcoming yellow. She reached into her handbag and after hunting around for a couple of pain killers found everything but. She remembered she had put a couple in her purse before going out as you never knows when you may need them, as she pulled out the painkillers she also pulled out the business card *James Harrington* she read again, funny she was starting work for Carrington's on Monday morning what a coincidence of the similar names, she sighed to herself how and why would anyone find her attractive and even if they did as soon as they found out anything about her life they would run a mile without looking back, must have been a bet from one of his friends, or a "who could pull the ugliest bird night" she agreed to herself. Nope she was better off alone, well she was never actually alone she had Daniel, her parents and she had Maddie, she was never one for making new friends way too shy that's how her and Maddie had become friends, the two of them both as shy as each other ended up spending the first week of playgroup joined at the hip clinging to each other for support, they had been best friends from then on as they made it through infant school, junior school and even when they hit their teenage years. Maddie's shyness was in the past but with Annette even though she was not as bad as she had been, shyness still prevented her from starting conversations with people she did not know very well, even standing outside the school gates, when Daniel had first started infant school she never really spoke to anyone else, Annette preferred to keep herself to herself and by the time Daniel had moved on to junior school the few times that she did try to make conversation to other friendly looking parents also waiting in the playground she never knew what to say, the other parents used to mutter a quick "hello" but as soon as they caught a glimpse of a black eye or bruise marks on her arm or leg they used to look away and seemed to avoid standing near her. Over the years Annette had learnt not to bother trying, she used to arrive at school just in time for the school bell going so Daniel used to come straight out and Annette had no need to talk to anyone else.

James Harrington he sounded like a right stuck up ponce!

She swallowed down the pain killers and had to admit he was actually rather good looking what she managed to see of him anyway, why he chose to come up to her she will never know after all men normally went up to Maddie and asked for her number instead and they just ignored Annette.

She told herself again that it must have been a bet from one of his friends, good thing she was not really interested.

Annette ripped up his business card and put it in the bin, 'Goodbye Mr Harrington' she said to herself as she threw the torn up bits of white card on top of yesterday's left over dinner, Annette drank down the last of her water and went back up to bed to try and get a bit more sleep, she crossed her fingers on the way up the stairs and hoped that next time she woke up she would be feeling a lot better.

At 11am Annette was woken up by the sound of the phone ringing, she heard Daniel answer it shortly followed by a gentle knock on her bedroom door.

'Mum, Mum' Daniel whispered 'you awake?'

'It's Maddie on the phone, she sounds rough' he said quietly as he passed her the phone.

'Hello you' came a husky voice at the other end of the phone.

Annette laughed 'Oh my gosh, Maddie, how much did we actually drink last night?'

'Not enough as I clearly remember everything including the knicker flasher girl.'

They both laughed at the memory.

'So' said Maddie when they had both finished laughing, 'You going to call Mr Dream boat man?'

'No' said Annette 'I threw his number in the bin, I'm not interested in him or any other man for that matter and you of all people should know that.'

'Sorry Annette, I know you say you're not interested but it's been a couple of years now and I just want you to be happy.'

'I am happy' Annette sighed, 'just me and Daniel just the way I like it.'

'Okay okay' said Maddie, 'what we doing today?'

'Want to meet up for a late breakfast?'

'Why not, what time?'

'It's just gone 11am now, say about 12.30?'

'Sounds good, how about we meet at that quiet little café off the High Street,'

'Sounds good see you then, bye,'

'Bye Hun' replied Maddie and they both hung up.

Annette stayed in bed five minutes more looking around her and sighed, yes she was happy she thought to herself. Her bedroom was now painted a pale pink with pink and silver pictures on the wall, she had upgraded to a king size bed with pink sheets with pink and silver curtains, the bed and furniture were nothing special but it was a nice quiet peaceful room just how she had always imagined it would be, Simon would have never let her have anything pink in the bedroom they used to share. The bedroom they used to share was green, his favourite colour, nothing was painted green in Annette's house and never would be, she finally felt herself here, she was relaxed, not a shadow of her former self, stressed daily, making sure the house was spotless, dinner ready and waiting for him, being careful what she said to him, only making phone calls when he allowed her to make them and the rest. She shook herself to get rid of the memories, got out of bed and went to the bathroom, she was safe here, happy here in her house, she actually slept all night now (apart from last) and of course she could decorate her house any way she liked as long as its tasteful the landlord had stated on the contract, other than Daniel's bedroom which was to be how he wanted it, he was almost nine years old when they had first moved back to the area where he had been born and the same area where Annette had grown up and now he was coming up eleven years old.

Daniel's room was his sanction, he had chosen the paint himself Annette did actually have to intervene and say no when he originally wanted to paint the whole room black but other than that it was down to him. He had eventually chosen a light fresh shade of blue and as Annette walked past Daniel's bedroom to get to the bathroom Daniel's bedroom door was open and the colour of his walls reminded her of the man's eyes last night! *James Harrington* she remembered his name. 'Stop it!' She quickly scolded herself you did very much the right thing by throwing his number in the bin, Annette asked Daniel if he wanted to join them for brunch, he declined and said he would rather stick pins in his eyes then sit with a couple of old gossipy women in some greasy café, what if his friends saw him with his mum how embarrassing, she playfully punched him on the arm and said 'who you calling old cheeky,' she showered and changed into a nice pair of jeans and her old favourite jumper and went off to meet Maddie.

Chapter Seven

It was a nice day, cold but sunny so Annette decided to walk to the café it was only a twenty minute walk and she needed to clear her head a bit, it was still a bit fuzzy from last night even though she had taken another couple of pain killers and decided the walk would do her good and perhaps she may even lose a bit of weight. Annette was not a large woman she was a nice size 12 but still had a bit of belly left after having Daniel, she had put on two stone during her pregnancy with him and had never managed to shift that last little bit of baby belly as she called it, she had tried; Simon used to tease her and taunt her about how fat she was, but now he was gone it had taken her a while but she no longer believed she was fat, in fact she liked being the size she was it was just the baby belly, she did keep meaning to join the gym but never quite got around to it.

James was awake with a raging hangover he looked around at where he was; cream walls, cream curtains and cream bed sheets he had stayed at Nathan's last night! By the side of him was a blonde haired woman (bleach blonde he noticed the darker roots showing through) she was still asleep, make up smudged all over the pillow, Nathan would not be happy about that nor would Kathleen if she saw it.

James got quietly and slowly out of bed, careful not to wake the sleeping woman and put his boxer shorts on that he picked up from the floor, he stepped over the red dress that was crumpled next to them, he walked in to the kitchen and groaned to himself why does he drink so much, his head was throbbing and his mouth was dry, cheap champagne always did that to him, not to mention the beer he had drank as well, as he poured himself a glass of orange juice, warm orange juice as someone had not put it back in the fridge before they had gone to bed after a few more drinks when they had got home. If he was sober he would never of ended up in bed with her, that was his trouble he usually did ever since Karen had gone off with Paul he had been like it, just one woman after the next, he looked out of the window and down to the pavement to where his silver Aston Martin was parked thankfully still there he had only had the car a few months but he loved it like it was a real person, if he had stayed at his last night then his Aston would have been safely tucked up in the underground car park with 24/7 security cameras and a man on the gates day and night. He turned around at the sound of a door opening and watched as a woman appeared in the doorway, she looked awful and he wondered what he ever found attractive about her in the first place, she was wearing Nathan's spare dressing gown that hung behind the door of the spare room he had stayed in. She asked if she could perhaps borrow a shirt or something as she did not bring any spare clothes, she had not planned on staying out the night and gave a little giggle, he put down his drink took one last look at his car and walked back into the bedroom, he gave her his shirt to put over her red dress and called her a cab, he was in no fit state to drive himself yet and wanted her gone before Nathan woke up. With promises to call her and to meet up again she finally left wearing his shirt, but not until after making sure he had her mobile number, home number, fax number and her email address, work and personal!

He watched her out of the window getting into the cab wearing his shirt she looked up and waved, he waved back muttering 'bye hope to never see you again!'

He heard the shower running, Nathan must be awake he put the kettle on to make a couple of strong black coffees and wondered if Nathan was interested in going out for a decent fry up.

Annette and Maddie were sitting in the café enjoying their late breakfast-early lunch, and sipping nice sweet hot cups of tea. The cafe they were at was nice and quiet down an alleyway in town and if you did not know it was there you would never tell, they did a full fry up for under four pounds which included two rounds of toast and pot of tea in the price. Annette had hers with extra crispy bacon, just as she had finished her last mouthful and was finishing up her tea her mobile phone rang, it was Daniel.

'Got no milk mum can you bring some home now?'

'Dan! Can't you go and buy some yourself' she replied,

'No it's too cold outside' he whined.

They had a small corner shop five minutes away from their house and it was not that cold outside.

'Alright' she sighed into the phone 'I will be back soon.'

Dan grunted something into the phone then hung up Annette guessed the grunt was a thank you mum.

Maddie looked up, 'Why could he not have gone and got the milk himself?'

'I don't know' shrugged Annette,

'You mother him too much' laughed Maddie.

'Come on then if you're finished I will give you a lift to the shop then drop you home.'

They paid and said how nice their food was, just what they had needed to clear the hangovers.

Annette could have done with spending another half hour in the café and perhaps another cup of tea, it was nice and warm in the cafe and she was enjoying the full up feeling in her stomach, her hangover had finally lifted and she felt great.

They walked along the High Street arm in arm giggling and going back through last night events and turned the corner in the direction of the car park.

James and Nathan were walking towards the café it was only a 10 min walk from Nathan's flat he had one of the new executive flats at the other end of the High Street next to James's apartment block, they were both too hung-over to drive and were probably very much still over the drink drive limit.

As Annette and Maddie turned the corner James stared at the back of the two girls who had just come out of the alleyway and he thought he recognised them, well at least the one on the right he was sure he had seen before, he stared at the back of Annette's head and noticed the way the sunlight shimmered off her beautiful hair.

'She looks like that that girl from last night' he said to Nathan, 'The one I gave my number too,'

'You not forgotten about her yet?' replied Nathan, 'After the noises that came from your room last night I'm surprised you can remember anything else,'

'Don't remind me' groaned James, 'And she left wearing my best shirt,'

'Never mind mate you can keep mine,'

Nathan looked at his best mate and laughed, James was wearing one of his shirts he had to lend him, it was actually a nice shirt it was just a bit on the small side, Nathan was not what you would class as skinny but James had a bit more muscle than him, Nathan was a touch taller and had blue eyes but they both had the same blonde hair.

Nathan and James had both met when they started secondary school, James had got picked on for wearing glasses, it was Nathan who came to rescue him, that's when their friendship had started, best friends through thick and thin other than the slight fall out when Nathan had kissed a girl at the year 9 school disco, he did not know that James had liked her as James had always been a bit shy when it came to the girls. Shortly after that James and Karen had got together and had stayed together until the end of high school when she ran off with Paul, that's when James changed, he started to work out and bulk himself up a bit, ditched the glasses and went for contacts but more importantly he no longer cared how he treated women, he never actually went out of his way to get a woman but they found him and he could not say no, Kathleen was not too keen on James after he had slept his way through a few of her friends she no longer tried to find a partner for him and begun to warn her friends not to go near him. Nathan knew how much the Karen business had upset James as he was the one who made the call to the ambulance the time he found James slumped on the bathroom floor after a cocktail of pain killers and alcohol, James was to Nathan the brother he never had and Nathan was the same to James.

James nudged Nathan in the ribs and did his jacket up so no one could see the shirt underneath, not that he really cared he was thinking about that girl he had seen just now, he was sure it was the girl from the nightclub he crossed his fingers that she would call.

It was now Sunday night and Annette was in a flap she was starting work tomorrow, she was going through her wardrobe while Daniel was in the bath and could not work out what to wear for work tomorrow; she had bought a couple of suits in between buying furniture and moving but was not sure which one to wear she wanted to make a good impression but did not want to wear the same outfit she had worn for the interview, she looked at her left wrist the bracelet was still there, she had not taken it off since Maddie had done it up on her wrist just before the interview.

Her life had gone into a full fast forward mode, job, car, house, Daniel had taken everything in his stride and Annette had promised him that yes his friends from school could come around for his birthday party, life was good, everything was good, her life, Daniel's life, her and Daniel's life, she had not heard anything from Simon since changing her mobile number and that's how she hoped it would stay she shuddered when she thought of Simon and picked up the phone to call Maddie for clothing advice.

Maddie finally left at 9pm after helping Annette organise a whole week's worth of smart work clothes, Annette had said goodnight to Daniel and tucked him into bed, he was going to be eleven years old in a few week's time and he was having a pizza and movie night in, she ran herself a hot bubble bath and took a glass of wine in the bathroom with her, just the one as she wanted to be fresh and alert for her first day Tomorrow, she was nervous and excited when she got into bed at 10 pm, that night her parents had rung while she was in the bath to wish her good luck and Maddie had promised to ring in the morning, she slept surprisingly well and woke sick with nerves, you will be fine said Maddie on the phone at 7.30 that morning, who had rung as promised while Annette was getting breakfast and packed lunches ready, she told Daniel to hurry up she was dropping him off at school on her way to work and she really did not want either of them being late. Neither were late, Annette had actually arrived early for her first day of work so she had time to re check her makeup and double check she had everything she needed for her first day, took a deep breath and walked in to sit behind what was now her desk in the middle of the vast reception/waiting area.

Chapter Eight

It was a few weeks after James Harrington had gone with Nathan to the nightclub, his real surname was Carrington but he liked going by Harrington as that way no one linked him with the family business as soon as they heard his name, he was now sitting in his front room, like Nathan he had a very nice apartment but unlike Nathan he had the penthouse suite (of course).

The whole flat was open plan, the kitchen was large with black cupboards along the wall, black granite work surfaces, built in washing machine, tumble dryer and dishwasher not that any of that ever got used in true bachelor style James ate most of his meals out or had a take away.

He had his washing laundered and ironed for him.

The black kitchen cupboards had no handles; they were operated by touch, smart chrome appliances lined the work surfaces not that he even knew how to use the juicer but it looked good for when he had people around, the most used appliance in the kitchen was the coffee machine any type of coffee you wanted at the touch of a button black with two sugars in James's case.

The kitchen had a long step down into the wooden floored living room where he had a black leather reclining sofa against the wall, two black leather lazy chairs either side of the sofa arranged in a semi-circle with his 42 inch black plasma pride of place in the middle on a black and chrome stand, a black glassed and chrome legged coffee table was the only other thing in the front room.

There was an archway which led out into the hall way, his front door was to the right and his office directly opposite the archway,

It was not so much of an office but more of a gaming room,

James had different gaming consoles and gaming chairs ready and waiting for the next time him and Nathan spent hours trying to beat each other's high score. He also had a football table one side of the room and he had a beer fridge installed in the wall.

Next to the games/office room was his bathroom he loved the shower that was in here it had a built in television with DVD, built in radio, back massage jets, room for two and even a foot massager in the floor of the shower. From the bathroom you could walk into James's bedroom as well as access it from a door in the corridor. His bedroom was black and cream, black silk bed sheets and black silk curtains covering the window to the right of the bed, the bed itself was a handmade king size solid oak bed, the wardrobes were all built in and he could sit in his bed and press a button on his remote and a panel built into the wall would slide back revealing another 42 inch television.

The control also had a button that opened and closed his curtains which were closed most of the time.

He could press another button to turn on the music system that played throughout the apartment with a speaker built in, in every room.

The whole apartment also had under floor heating that was controlled by remote.

The best part about the whole apartment was the fact it was free, free rent, free utility bills all James had to pay for was his food.

While James was busy growing up, his parents had made a fortune in the property market buying old houses that were falling apart knocking them down and building large family homes with all the comforts and mod con's you could want.

They also bought run down blocks of flats and turned them into executive flats (like the one James lived in himself) for the young working yuppie city types who commuted to

London every day or like him lived off mummy and daddy's hard earned money.

James did not have to work, his parent's had made him chairman of the business when they had retired, his parents now lived abroad and like himself lived off the business hence the free rent and free utility bills, they were not actually free, the monthly payments came out of the business accounts which was now run by some of the top advisors in the UK, which is why James, never had to work.

Occasionally he had to turn up to company meetings he um'd and ar'd in the right places and shook his head when everyone else did, everyone else made the decisions for him so there was never really any need for him to say or do anything at all.

Of course being chairman of a multi million pound company came with a huge pay packet, with no rent to pay he spent most of it on girls, partying and eating out.

He enjoyed himself but it was at times like this when he was on his own in the quietness of his apartment with just his own company, he wished he had someone else to share everything he had, he had plenty of women he could have called any of them right now and they would be there like a shot with or without a friend depending on what he wanted,

They all loved the money but none of them actually knew the real him.

James was not really interested in girls like that, yes he has a laugh with them and they look good on his arm and of course they were good in the bedroom department but he could not imagine himself marrying any of them or experiencing any of them having his children, he takes them out for meals and all they ever eat is salad, even then they leave half of their meal claiming to be full up and could not eat another thing, yet they all somehow manage to wash what little they had eaten down with a couple of bottles of Louis Roederer Cristal or Dom Perignon Oenotheque which was always paid for by him or in his case paid by the swipe of his black am-ex card, after the meal it was always back to his apartment for a night of mind blowing sex, or in some cases just sex, followed by a morning conversation consisting of promises to call them and agreeing how they were the best lover he had ever had, calling them a cab kissing them goodbye and then never seeing them again. He knew that was not how he wanted to be but it's how he was, he often wondered where and when he would meet a decent woman whom he could love and cherish, spoil rotten, shower with love and get the same in return, he would respect her and have a family with her and spend the rest of his life in the happy ever after like his parents have. He shook his head he would never meet a woman like that they all just wanted him for his money and for what they could get out him, a free ride his father once said after meeting one of his many floozies, he wanted a woman his parents would love as much as he did, he would never find anyone like that he sighed to himself.

It was coming to the end of another working week for Annette in her new job and she loved it, Maddie had actually needed to hire a third person to fill the gap that Annette had left so Maddie could spend more of her time designing new clothes rather than just selling them.

As promised Annette was having Daniel's friends around Friday (tomorrow) night for his birthday and then herself and Daniel were going bowling Saturday afternoon, then out to dinner in the evening with her mum, dad and Maddie, and Annette *was* paying.

She had put aside a bit of money each week from her last three weeks of wages to make sure she had enough money to cover all the boring things she had had to pay as well as the meal, this meal was going to be a toast to Daniel for his eleventh birthday, a thank you to her parents and Maddie as well as a congratulations for getting the new job. Annette finished work at 5.00pm on the dot and hurried to the supermarket, she still had to get Daniel's birthday cake, crisps, a couple bottles of coke caffeine free she decided as a house full of hyped up ten and eleven year olds was not her idea of fun. She walked through the doors and looked around, why when she was in a hurry the world and his wife decided to go shopping! The queues were long and children were screaming, Annette took a deep breath grabbed a basket and went in search for the goodies she needed, she was standing down the cake isle deciding whether to go for a chocolate cake or double chocolate cake when she felt someone standing beside her.

'You never called' she heard a male voice say.

She decided to go for the double chocolate cake and reached out to take one for her basket.

A hand landed gently on her shoulder. Annette froze.

'You never called.' said the voice again.

As Annette turned she looked into the speaker's eyes, they were the brightest green she had ever seen they were shining and Annette felt herself blush and then she felt her stomach drop, it was him, him, that man, the man from the club, James or whatever his name was.

'Oh' Annette stammered out, James was standing right in front of her now.

'My dog ate your number' she blurted out then felt her cheeks flush, why did I say that she scolded herself of all the stupid things to say!

James was smiling at her now, he did have a gorgeous smile, Annette felt a stirring inside her, something she had not felt for a while, a long while, it was lust!

'I must go' she said when she finally spoke which seemed like hours later, 'Need to get home, birthday party.'

'Nice to see you again' James replied.

'Yes' said Annette 'Goodbye then.'

She almost ran off back down the aisle towards the checkout, in fact she was walking fast with her heart pounding, oh my gosh what must I have looked like she thought as she smoothed down her hair with her hands, oh no the basket, she had put the basket down in the aisle after realising who the man was, she turned around cheeks hot and flushed with embarrassment and looked back down the aisle she had just walked from, James was still standing where he was when she had said goodbye, he was holding her basket in his hand, she followed the line of his arm and noticed he had tanned and toned arms, she swallowed took a deep breath and walked back towards him.

'Hi' James said when she reached him.

'Hi' Annette said back she was feeling rather stupid like she had walked out of a public toilet with her skirt tucked in to her knickers.

'I believe this is yours' said James with a laugh as he handed over her basket.

Annette looked at the floor as she took the basket from him as their fingers touched Annette felt like she had just melted through the floor

'Thank you' she managed to say.

'May I ask what you name is?' enquired James.

'I'm Annette' she replied.

James held out his hand 'very pleased to meet you Annette I am James,' he said as he held out his hand for her to shake. Annette gave a girly giggle as she shook his hand after all it would have been rude just to grab the basket and run as fast as she could away from him, even though that's what her head was screaming at her to do.

'Good choice on the cake' James said as he looked into her basket.

'It's for my son' Annette said as a way of an explanation. 'It's his birthday tomorrow, He is having a few friends around this evening and if I don't get going soon I will end up with a gang of boys on my door step, wondering what kind of mother I am to not even be there when they arrive.'

'It was nice meeting you again Annette and if you don't mind me saying, the lighting in the night club did nothing for you, you are much more beautiful than I remember,'

Annette felt herself blush all over again 'nice meeting you again too James' as she turned and walked back down the aisle this time *with* her basket in her hand, she managed to find a checkout that was empty, she looked at her watch it was 6.30 pm, Daniel's friends were due around in an hour and her parents would be wondering where she had got to, she paid and hurried to her car, she put the shopping in the boot and pulled out her phone to call her mother. She was just telling her mum she was on her way, when from the safety of her car she watched James leaving the supermarket, he was tall and tanned and he looked like every muscle on his body was toned, he was wearing a white t-shirt and a pair of dark blue jeans with black loafers on his feet, he walked tall and with confidence, 'are you still there' came a voice from the phone. 'Annette?' said her mother's voice.

'Gosh sorry mum yes still here must have lost reception a bit there; I'm on my way so see you in about 10 minutes.'

As Annette hung up she looked around for James again but he had gone.

Annette and Daniel had, had a great evening, Annette silently vowed never to have a sleep over again, she was shattered. Daniel and his friends had not gone to sleep much before 1am neither had Annette, she could hear them chattering and laughing through the floorboards, she had let the boys all sleep on the front room floor as it was the biggest space in the house, the boys had really enjoyed themselves and had all gone home by 11am the next day, giving Annette time to tidy up the mess they had all made and get ready for their 1pm bowling, she was looking forward to spending some time with Daniel, what with the house move and a full time job, she was not sure how much time they would have to spend together now, the afternoon flew by they were having so much fun. Daniel won with seven games to Annette's three, her arm ached after so many games but it was worth it, they went and had a snack after finishing their last game to celebrate Daniel's win, but only a snack, as Annette was looking forward to tonight's meal. It was 5pm, her parents were coming around at 7pm and they were meeting Maddie at the restaurant bar around 7.30pm with the table booked for 8pm. Daniel had a quick shower while Annette was standing in her bedroom, wardrobe door wide open and she was pulling out different tops and trousers, different skirts, cardigans, shirts, and shoes all scattered over her bed and bedroom floor.

'Bathroom's free' called out Daniel.

'Thanks love' shouted back Annette and sighed to herself, she really did not know what to wear, in the end Daniel chose the outfit for her. Annette had a quick soak in a nice hot bubble bath and she shaved where she needed too. After lathering on moisturising cream to stop her legs coming out in a shaving rash she got dressed in the outfit Daniel had chosen for her and they left the house on time to meet with her parents and Maddie.

Chapter Nine

It was Sunday afternoon; James was due into the office on Monday for another routine meeting. The meeting was to start at 5pm sharp so he was told. He was getting bored of his playboy lifestyle and the closer it got to Nathan's wedding day the less he saw of his closest friend. James sighed as he thought about his chance meetings with Annette, first in the supermarket with her looking all cute and harassed and then again last night in the restaurant when she looked, well, wow! was the only way he could describe her, his heart soared when he saw her walk in, he was sitting in a corner away from the doors so he could still see who was coming in and out which was a good thing as he was waiting for Tom. Tom worked at Carrington's as manager, he was also a close friend of the family and James's Godfather; James was watching the doors waiting for Tom to join him when Annette walked in, she was wearing dark blue jeans and a simple white strappy top, her hair shone and fell gently around her face resting on her shoulders. She was sitting next to a boy who looked around twelve years old, whom he guessed was her son and her friend with the blonde hair whom he had seen in the club with Annette the first time they had met, she looked happy and content he thought, she was smiling and laughing, her laughter carried over to the table where he was sitting waiting for Tom.

He never asked for her number in the supermarket and never gave her his number again either, at least she must live in the same area he thought, perhaps they will bump into each other again and then he could ask for her number, He had toyed with the idea of going over but it looked like a family gathering and he did not want to embarrass himself in front of her, he smiled to himself as he noticed the only man at the table was a lot older than Annette herself and he was sitting next to an older woman. James hazarded a guess that it was Annette's parents sitting at the table with them and if that was Annette's son as James was assuming he was, they may not take too kindly to a strange man asking for her number in front of him. Perhaps Annette's husband would be joining them later he reasoned with himself, he had not noticed a ring on her left hand but then again he had not really looked, he was far too busy staring at her kind, smiling face; she did say her dog had eaten his business card and never mentioned anything about a man being around.

The doors to the restaurant had opened again and finally this time Tom walked in.

'Sorry I'm late had a bit of trouble at the office' Tom said as he reached James's table.

'We must be paying our employees too much' he joked to James, 'I'm sure I just noticed our new receptionist dining here.'

James just nodded back in agreement without even looking at who Tom was talking about, he was too busy looking over at Annette wondering if she was single or not and how much he wished she was actually single. James was not too sure if he even knew they had a new receptionist, oh well he would find out on Monday, whoever she was he hoped she was better than the young thing whom they had to fired, she had spent far too much time making personal calls rather than taking note of their client's needs.

Annette was having a great evening, the food was divine, the restaurant itself was relaxing, a small little Italian place just off the High Street in town, her father was making so many jokes her face hurt from smiling and laughing so much, this was the best birthday Daniel had ever had Annette had thought. Daniel was relaxed and was laughing along with everyone else at the table even though at one point Annette needed to tell her father off for some of the jokes that she did not feel suitable for Daniel's ears, but as she told her father off she was only half serious and her dad knew it, but he did tone down the next few jokes for her benefit. They had shared two garlic breads with cheese for a starter, her father was eating a pasta dish, her mother had the fish which she said was the best meal she'd ever had and asked her husband why they did not eat here more often. Daniel and Annette had already shared a pizza and were now enjoying spaghetti bolognaise, Daniel had decided he was having ice cream for dessert. After finishing her main course she asked her parents to order her a coffee while she nipped to the loo. Quick hair and makeup check in the mirror, then back to the table, Annette almost bumped into someone on the way out, 'oh sorry' Annette said as she looked up into James's eyes, 'oh' Annette blushed.

'Hi' said James.

'Oh, hi' stammered out Annette, 'I'm out for my son's birthday, must get back to the table or they will be wondering where I have gone, bye.'

'Yes bye' was all James managed to reply back, 'nice seeing you again' Annette replied as she scurried away.

James thought as he left the restaurant, she really was a lovely looking woman and she said son's birthday, so far he was at least right about one thing.

'You ok love' her mum asked as she sat back at the table, 'you're looking very flushed.'

'I'm fine mum, must have been the hand dryer' Annette lied, she hated lying but how could she tell them the truth, she was flushed due to the fact she had just bumped into the most gorgeous man she had ever met "again."

As her coffee arrived Annette sat there staring at it reminding herself over and over again that she was not interested in the slightest in that man, never had been and never would be.

Annette's mum looked over at Annette with a quizzical look on her face, Annette looked away and asked her father to tell another one of his jokes. With James pushed to the back of her mind, they finished their perfect evening and laughed and joked all the way back to the car park. It was after 10pm when they finally arrived home, Daniel went straight to bed; Annette had invited her parents and Maddie back but they declined seeing as it was late and Annette and Maddie had work in the morning.

Annette made herself a warm mug of milk and sat at her kitchen table where she replayed her encounter with James over and over in her head until at midnight she finally went up to bed with a warm fuzzy glow in her tummy which she put down to the warm milk, her heart was saying otherwise but Annette decided to ignore that.

Monday morning, Annette awoke and groaned when the alarm went off, she had not slept very well, the more she tried not to think about James, the more she thought about him, she called to Daniel and they both got ready and left the house on time.

James was still asleep, he had been thinking about Annette for most of the evening, he really had to find a way of contacting her but he did not even know where she worked or if she worked at all for that matter. He had guessed she lived in the same area as him due to the chance meetings they'd had, he just wished he knew more about her, other than she was called Annette and she had a son.

Annette got to work right on time and got on with the work she had to do, she rang Maddie on her lunch break and told her all about her meeting with James, Maddie laughed 'it sounds like u have a crush, a bad crush,' which made Annette blush.

'Ok maybe I have a small crush' confessed Annette 'but that is as far as it can go, you know I am not interested in anyone.'

'Not even a man with such gorgeous eyes as him.'

'Not even him' replied Annette with her fingers crossed.

James woke up at midday, looked at his clock and sighed, he had to be at a work meeting at 5pm and he was not looking forward to it. After Tom had given him a bollocking about not taking the job or business seriously he had decided to make more of an effort, after all without the business he would not have the apartment or the car.

Annette got back to her desk at 1pm to find Claire her work colleague waiting for her.

'We got Daniel a little something for his birthday, hope you don't mind' said Claire handing Annette a small neatly wrapped present.

'Thank you, you shouldn't have,' Annette said as she tucked the present under her desk for safe keeping until it was 5pm when Annette left for the day.

'Big boss in for a meeting this afternoon' whispered Claire.

'Don't remind me; I will probably get the sack on the spot for being too old as soon as he lays eyes on me.'

'Don't be silly Annette' said Claire 'he will love you just as much as we do and if it makes you feel any better he is more your age than ours so he can't, and if he did we would all go on strike then where would he be, anyway he is never around, he just leaves us to run the business for him, so he would be stuffed without us,' cooed Claire.

Claire worked up on the first floor in a management position. She was only twenty two years of age, like most of the others who worked in the same building, other than Tom who had been one of the people who had interviewed Annette for her role in the company.

'You probably won't even see him, the meeting is meant to start at 5pm but he is always late.'

'Right I best get back to work, see you soon Annette and before I forget to tell you some of us girls are going out on Friday night if you want to join us for a few drinks,'

'Not sure if I can' replied Annette 'but thanks anyway.'

Annette got back on with her work and before she knew it, it was almost 5pm; she was just shutting down her laptop when Tom came over, 'Hi Annette, how are you enjoying the new job?'

'Hi Tom, the job's going fine thank you and how are you today?'

'Other than waiting for Mr Big Shot himself I am fine' laughed Tom.

'Yes I heard he was coming in today' said Annette unable to think of anything else to say.

Tom looked at his jacket; 'damn' he exclaimed quite loudly 'must have spilt some lunch down my jacket' as he brushed at the stain with his hands.

'Here, try this' said Annette putting her handbag on the desk and pulling out a packet of baby wipes,'

'Thanks Annette, you certainly can tell you are a mother,' grinned Tom as he started trying to clean up the mark on his jacket. 'Are you just leaving?' 'I will walk to the door with you. I am going to wait for him outside'

Annette nodded a yes to Tom as she grabbed her handbag off the desk and walked outside with him.

'If that man is not here in a minute the meeting will have to start without him' sighed Tom, 'why can't he just be on time for once!'

Annette judged by the tone of his voice that being on time was not something her big boss was used to doing.

'I am sure he will be' remarked Annette, 'see you tomorrow' Annette headed off to the car park, leaving Tom pacing up and down outside the main doors.

Annette got into her car and was about to drive off, 'shit!' Annette exclaimed out loud to herself, she had forgotten Daniel's gift she had to get back out of her car to go back in the office and get it out from under her desk where she had been keeping it safe. As she walked back into the building she noticed Tom was no longer outside, her boss had got to the meeting on time or he was late and Tom had given up on him Annette decided, Annette also hoped her boss was already in she did not fancy bumping into him.

Annette got to her desk and bent underneath to pick up the present.

'So this is where you have been hiding,' said a male voice.

Thump!

The voice had startled Annette, she knew straight away whom it belong to. 'Ouch' exclaimed Annette rubbing the top of her head and sitting back up straight in her chair she looked right into those stunning green eyes again.

'Oh sugar! I am so sorry I did not mean to scare you Annette' said James worriedly, 'does it hurt badly, there's no blood is there? Want me to take a look?'

'No, no I am fine,' 'what are you doing here anyway?'

'I have a meeting with a man named Tom, do you know him and have you seen him anywhere?'

'Yes I do know a Tom, Tom Moore? 'If it is Tom Moore you're asking about then he is my boss and the last time I saw him he was waiting outside for our main boss when I left; I forgot my son's gift so came back in for it, which is why I am here now,' Annette gestured her arms around the main reception area, 'And then he was gone' she continued. 'So I hope for my main boss's sake that means the meeting started on time with him in there, Actually' continued Annette 'If you're attending the same meeting then, you're late, it started' Annette glanced down at the watch on her wrist 'twenty minutes ago,'

'Never mind, I don't think they will be too cross with me I have a property for them all to look at,'

'Is that what you do?' enquired Annette 'deal with properties?'

'Yes and I think Tom and Co. would be very interested to get their hands on this one,' grinned James.

'Well I hope the main boss and Tom both like it,' blushed Annette. She felt her insides turn to jelly when James grinned at her, she could see the sparkle in his eyes and her heart began to beat a funny kind of rhythm.

'I take it you work here?' enquired James leaning forward onto Annette's desk.

'Yup right here,' she replied patting the desk then backing away from where James was now leaning. She could smell him, it was a mixture of shower gel and aftershave, a kind of clean musky smell, it was making Annette want to breathe the smell in and savour it, 'I have only been here a few months and really enjoy working here, shouldn't you be getting to the meeting you don't want to be any later' smiled Annette.

'Yes, your right, I had better be off, see you soon?' Annette had a feeling that last remark was more of a question than a goodbye it made her blush again.

'Yes see you soon' smiled Annette 'and good luck for the meeting, hope big boss likes it.'

This time Annette checked she had everything, handbag, keys, Daniel's present, and hurried out of the building, she really did not want to stay any longer she was still fearful of bumping into her main boss just in case he was running late and not already in the meeting as she had hoped. As she got in her car she thought; if her bosses did like the property did that mean she would be seeing James more often, she hoped not she told herself, but her heart swelled with that idea, *stop it* she ordered herself as she eased her car out of the car park, *your behaving like a love struck teenager* she told herself, as a silly grin worked its way across her face.

James went up in the lift with a big grin spreading across his face and made a mental note to have some flowers delivered to her first thing, he knew Tom would not be happy he was late again but he felt like he was floating down the corridor to the board room door.

'You will never guess who I bumped into' squealed Annette, she had phoned Maddie as soon as she'd got home and invited her over once Daniel had gone to bed, Annette had said she would spill the beans when she got there.

'Who, tell me all' laughed Maddie when she had arrived.

'It was him' said Annette with a sigh.

'Him, as in the delicious James that you are *sooooo* not interested in' enquired Maddie.

'I am *not* interested in him!' she looked at Maddie who was now looking at Annette with one eyebrow raised.

'Ok well maybe I am, but only a little bit.' Maddie still had one eyebrow raised as she looked at Annette, 'Okay, okay maybe a lot' confessed Annette.

'Now that's more like it, I knew you liked him from the start, it's about time you admitted it to yourself,' with that confession out of the way the girls both fell about laughing.

Annette awoke early the next morning, she looked at the clock, I have half an hour before the alarm goes off she thought. She laid in bed and stared at the ceiling, a big grin worked its way across her face, she thought about meeting James yesterday, before she knew it, it was time to turn the alarm off and she sprung out of bed. Annette decided to make a bit more of an effort with her clothes and make-up for work this morning, nothing to do with the fact James maybe around of course she told herself.

At 7.30am just as she was ready to leave she received a text on her phone it was from Maddie, Annette laughed as she read: *Go for it girl*, Annette text back *lol* followed by a kiss,

'Come on Daniel let's go.' Called Annette,

'What's got into you today mum? you have been smiling all morning and I'm sure you don't normally wear your hair like that for work.'

'I'm just in a good mood today that's all'

'It's not your birthday and I have forgotten is it mum?'

Annette looked at Daniel's serious face and laughed,

'No darling it's not my birthday, like I said I am just in a good mood,' as Annette locked the door behind them, Daniel watched his mum, she was happy and it suited her, Daniel had heard some of his mum's conversation in the kitchen last night when she was talking to Maddie, he had heard the name James mentioned a few times, whoever this man was he was having a good effect on his mum as long as he did not hurt her in any way he did not really mind, if however he did hurt her. Daniel had agreed to himself that he would never let another man hurt his mother the way his dad had done, ever again and he meant it.

Chapter Ten

Annette arrived at 8:50am she was ten minutes early so had decided to sit in her car for a bit, she could not sit still her mind was wandering. What would she say to James if he was there in the lobby or standing at her desk, what would she say if he came in at lunchtime, she checked her appearance in the mirror for the umpteenth time and reapplied her lipstick, not that it needed touching up as she had redone it again not that long ago. She watched as a delivery driver pulled up outside the main door and left the van with the biggest bunch of flowers she had ever seen, lucky girl she thought to herself and made a mental note to buy some for herself on the way home. She waited until the driver had left before walking into the office building, she saw the flowers on her desk they really were gorgeous, she saw Claire going over to them, must be for her Annette thought.

'Oh what lovely flowers' she said to Claire as she walked behind her desk, 'Who are they from?'

'That's what I would like to know' said Claire.

'Do they not say?'

'Nope it just says nice to see you again, I was hoping you could tell me who they were from.'

'Me' said Annette slightly confused, 'why would I know who they are from?'

Claire looked at her like she was a green monster from out of space then laughed 'read the card Annette, they are not for me, they are yours.'

'Mine.'

'Yes yours take a look.'

To Annette, nice to see you again, was all the card read, she felt her cheeks flush as she read it, she knew who the flowers were from.

'So' enquired Claire 'who sent you the most gorgeous bunch of flowers I have ever seen.'

'Just someone I bumped into a couple of times.'

'I wish I could bump into someone who would send me flowers like that' sighed Claire 'but right now I best get back upstairs before every one wonders if I have run off with the post,' you're such a lucky girl Annette.

'I know' giggled Annette as she reached into her bag for her phone to text Maddie with the news straight away.

'No way' said Maddie to Annette when they met up for lunch later that day. 'Oh they are lovely, must have cost him a fortune' as Maddie held the flowers in her hands.

'I know do you think I should call him and say thanks.'

'I think you should do more than that, I think you should invite him out for a drink to say thank you in person, and before you say you can't, I will have Daniel for you so you can have the evening free, now you have no excuse,'

'But,'

'No buts just do it!' Maddie demanded

'Okay, I will call him later, but what if he says he is busy.'

'Don't be silly; make it a Friday or Saturday evening so neither of you have work the next morning, I am sure he will say yes, don't you worry about that, I just have a feeling it will all work out.' Later that evening as Annette sat in the front room of her house, Daniel was still at a friend's but was due back at 8pm she looked at the clock above the fireplace 7.28pm the hands read, the house was quiet. She picked up the phone with a shaking hand and tried to dial the number, her heart was beating wildly in her chest; she was two digits away from dialling his whole number when she quickly put the phone down. You're being silly she told herself, you're just calling someone to say thank you for something they had given you, something lovely. Annette smiled as she looked at the flowers now standing in a pale blue vase, in the middle of her coffee table in the front room, 'right!' she told herself out loud, and took a deep breath and started to redial his number, the phone started to ring. Oh no its going to end up on an answer phone then what do I say, she began to quietly panic, just as Annette was about to hang up a breathless man's voice answered, 'Hello' the voice enquired,

'Hello' replied Annette as she tried to keep the wobble in her voice under control, 'It's me, Annette, I am just calling to say thank you for the flowers, they are so lovely, so, thank you again.'

'You're more than welcome and I am so glad you like them,'

'I was just wondering' stammered Annette now getting incredibly nervous; what if he says no sang a voice in her head.

'Yes?' James replied.

'Well, what I mean is' there was silence at the other end, she knew he was still there, she could hear him breathing, 'can you, well would you, let me take you out for a drink sometime to say thank you properly?' there she had said it, please say yes the voice in her head was now saying, say yes, say yes, say yes.

'That would be great' James finally replied, Annette let out a silent sigh of relief.

'When were you thinking of?'

'Oh erm I don't know' came Annette's truthful response,

'Well let's start with when are you available.' laughed James,

'Anytime' then Annette blushed as she realised what she had said, 'What I mean is after work I am normally free in the evenings,'

'What about this weekend.'

'This weekend' Annette managed to squeak, it was a Tuesday now, that only left three more days till the weekend. 'Actually this weekend I believe I am free' she replied as she finally recomposed herself, he must think I am a right loon she thought.

'Friday, Saturday?' James asked,

'Saturday' Annette confirmed; then she would not have to worry about rushing home from work. That would give her the whole day to get ready,

'Ok Saturday it is then, I look forward to it, shall we say 7.30pm, I can pick you up from yours if you like,'

'I can meet you at 7.30pm outside the train station in town, that would be easier for me, my house is a bit difficult to find' Annette did not know why she said that it was the first thing that came in to her head. In fact she did not want Daniel to know his mother was going off out for a drink with another man. She really did not think it would be a good idea for James to turn up on the door step.

'No problems 7.30pm outside the station it is, look forward to seeing you then' James said.

'Me too' said Annette and she really meant it.

'Bye for now,'

'Bye James.' Annette put the phone down the smile that had been spreading across her face during the call now filled most of her face; I did it she thought to herself, I really did it she squealed out loud.

The next few days flew by and she woke up on Saturday morning, to the sun shining through her window, the birds singing and a smile already on her face. Maddie was due around at 10am, they were going shopping for something Annette could wear this evening for her drink with James. She showered and tried to eat some breakfast, Daniel watched his mother from across the table, 'you ok mum?'

'Yes darling just not very hungry that's all,'

'What time is Maddie coming?'

'In about half hour' replied Annette as she checked her watch.

'I don't have to come, do I mum. Can I stay at home?'

'Just behave yourself while I am gone, and don't open the front door to anyone unless you know it's one of your friends,'

'Don't worry mum, I know the rules. I was just going to play on my computer anyway, I am on the last level now, then I would have completed the game and you will have to buy me a new one,'

'We will see about that' smiled Annette at her son, 'what game is it your after then' she said as she got up and grabbed a pen and paper to make a note of it, 'no promises though,'

'Of course not mum' but they both knew by the end of the day he would have the game he wanted.

True to her word Maddie turned up half an hour later, 'you ready to hit the shops,'

'As ready as I will ever be,' replied Annette.

'Bye Dan' she called over her shoulder,

'Bye mum, don't forget my game' he shouted from upstairs.

'I said we will see, remember!'

'Yes mum it's called Dragon Times, just in case of course.'

She smiled at Maddie, 'kids'! She exclaimed and they both laughed closing the door behind them.

It was just after 4pm by the time Annette had got home. Maddie and Annette were sitting in the kitchen exhausted and with sore feet, surrounded by bags of various sizes and colours, all of them holding items of clothing. Annette's purse was now quite a few pounds lighter than it had been when she had left this morning. As a surprise Maddie had booked Annette into the hairdressers so instead of her long straight dark hair, Annette now had a head of soft curls with a hint of lighter brown highlights, Maddie had insisted she paid for the hair cut and re style, so therefore Annette had to half drag Maddie through the door of the nail bar and had ordered them both a manicure and a pedicure and paid for them both as a thank you. Annette felt good and Maddie had to keep slapping Annette's hand away every time she reached up to touch her new curly head of hair. When they came home Daniel ran down the stairs to greet them and stopped with his mouth forming in an O shape when he saw his mum, 'Wow! Who are you and what have you done with my real mother?'

'Very funny' laughed Annette 'as I am not your *real* mother you won't be wanting this then' as she reached inside one of her many shopping bags and pulled out a small square package in a small carrier bag.

'Oh mum great you got me the game!' Daniel said as he took the bag from her hands and turned to run back up the stairs, he turned back around and gave his mum a huge hug, 'Thanks mum, you're the best and your hair really looks great, it really suits you, you know.'

'Thanks Daniel, go on, be off with you, if you're good you and Maddie can have a take away tonight,'

'New game and take away, you really must get your hair done more often' replied Daniel as he made his way back up the stairs.

'So' enquired Maddie 'which of the stunning new outfits are you going to wear tonight?'

'I have no idea Maddie; can I not just wear my jeans and t-shirt?'

'No you most certainly cannot, now let's get started' Maddie told Annette excitedly while unpacking the outfits and draping them across the kitchen chairs.

It was now 6.30pm and the nerves had kicked in, in full force, Annette had decided to wear a pale pink strapless top, white fitted trousers and a cute pair of white kitten heels. She had somehow managed to have a warm bath, without getting her hair wet, and it was a warm bath as she did not want any frizzy-ness to ruin the soft curls the hairdresser has produced, she buffed her skin and moisturised it with a product of Maddie's that left a soft shimmer on her skin, her toes and finger nails were still perfect. She got dressed and spritz on her favourite perfume, took one last look in her bedroom mirror and walked downstairs.

'Twit twoo' Whistled Maddie.

'I thought you were just meeting someone for a drink' commented Daniel.

'I am' replied Annette.

Daniel looked at her with his eyebrows raised 'And he is just a friend' he enquired.

'Yes my darling he is just a friend, you don't mind me having male friends do you?'

'No I don't mind mum, but if he ever lays a finger on you, he will have me to deal with!'

Annette watched as her eleven year old son puffed himself up like a peacock and a tear formed in her eye, she brushed her tear away and crouched down to where Daniel was sitting at the kitchen table, 'I will never let another man treat me like that again, you and me Daniel, I promise you he is just a friend, I don't intend on anything further, right now, you and my work mean everything to me, you first, work second and if anytime is left then a little bit for me,' she kissed the top of her son's head gently and enveloped him in a hug,

'Alright, alright, that's enough I am not five anymore you know mum,'

Annette pulled back and laughed, when had he grown from boy to almost a teenager it seemed not that long ago he used to love his mum's cuddles and kisses.

'Right 7pm I best get going, are you sure you will both be ok?' as she looked at Maddie.

'Yes we will be fine won't we Daniel, I have a handful of take away menus and enough bars of chocolate to last a week, you look great by the way.'

'Yer you really do mum, enjoy yourself won't you mum it's about time you did something for yourself.'

Annette stood up and smoothed down her trousers 'I won't be back late, no later than 9pm for your bed Mr,'

'Oh but mum' whined Daniel.

'That's ok isn't it Daniel! I will make sure he is tucked up and asleep by 9pm' said Maddie as she not so subtly winked at Daniel.

Annette tutted and laughed, 'Ok 10pm but that's final.'

'*Yessss*, great mum, thank you and mum…..'

'Yes Daniel,'

'Love you,'

'And I love you too Daniel.'

Annette walked out of the house, closed the door and sat in the car for a moment, how could she be leaving Daniel to go out with another man, maybe she should cancel, on second thoughts, Maddie would kill her or frog march her to meet James, so instead she took a deep breath and started her car.

James was in a bit of a flap after trying on half his wardrobe and throwing most of it on the floor, he decided to wear a pair of dark blue jeans that were also smart enough to pass as a pair of trousers; he chose a grey and white striped shirt and put on a pair of black shoes. He would take the car and park it; park it where? Or should he walk? No he would take the car and park it in the car park behind the station, he could always get a cab home if he ended up drinking one too many, it was 7pm he had best get a move on, and no way did he want to be late, not tonight.

It was 7.25pm Annette was in a traffic jam, the traffic lights were not working, she only had one more road to go before she turned in to the road that led to the station car park, she drummed her fingers on the steering wheel and checked her watch, 7.28pm, oh no she thought I really hope he waits for me.

James drove into the station car park at 7.22pm it had only taken him twenty minutes to get there. He was glad he was driving the other way as he had seen a huge backlog of cars thanks to the traffic lights no longer working. He pulled into a space, checked his appearance in the car mirror, popped a chewing gum in his mouth, parked the car and walked down the alleyway that led to the station.

At 7.36pm Annette pulled into a parking space in the station car park another spritz of perfume and she got out of the car, a car parked a few cars down from where she had parked caught her eye, it was a silver Aston Martin no less, lucky bugger she thought to herself. I wonder how much they have to earn to afford one of them, it probably belongs to some middle aged man, balding with bad breath who attends swingers parties with his poor dowdy wife; I may not have a lot she thought to herself but at least I'm happy and with that thought, she walked out of the car park and hurried along to the station.

'Oh gosh I am so sorry I am late,' she half panted when she had almost reached James, I got stuck in a stupid traffic jam, she looked at James who was just staring at her, she felt herself blush a dark crimson, and looked down at her shoes to avoid his stare.

Wow! was the first thought that entered his head before he managed to say 'your hair, it looks great, you look great,'

'Thank you, you don't look to bad yourself' she responded shyly.

They stood there just staring at each other for what felt like hours but it was only thirty seconds or so before James finally broke the silence 'so which direction are we heading in?' he asked Annette.

'Oh I don't know' she had not thought that far ahead and felt a bit stupid.

'Why don't we walk up the High Street and just see where our feet take us.'

Straight to your bed, Annette's head said, then she blushed at the thought and scolded herself, your just friends she reminded herself sternly, just friends.

'Yes that's a good idea' just friends she told herself again as they strolled up the road side by side.

'So you work at Carrington's then?'

'Yes I do, I have only been there a few months but so far so good, how did your meeting with Tom go the other afternoon?'

'Oh that went great they loved the property I showed them,'

'It looks like I might be seeing a lot of you then,'

'Would that be such a bad thing' laughed James.

'Oh no that's not what I meant' started Annette then she looked at James and he was smiling at her.

It made her tummy do a couple of somersaults, that smile and the way his eyes twinkled with laughter.

'Not fair' said Annette and nudged him playfully in the ribs James stumbled and held on to his ribs like Annette had just broken them, they both looked at each other and laughed.

James loved the way you could see her dimples every time she smiled and that her eyes were bright and playful.

'How about here?' James said as he caught Annette gently by the arm to stop her from walking on, they were standing outside a nice looking wine bar.

'Why not' said Annette and in they went.

It turned out to be a very nice little place, they had soft lighting, tables and chairs as well as a few sofas set opposite each other with a low table in between, and it was in these sofa's they chose to sit opposite one another, the sofas were leather and surprisingly comfortable.

'What will you have?' James enquired.

'A white wine spritzer, please, but you must let me pay for the drinks, after all we are here as a thank you to you for the flowers,'

'Ok' said James 'but you must let me buy the next round, make mine a pint of lager.'

Annette walked to the bar, James watched the way her bum wiggled in the tight white trousers, it was a nice bottom James thought, the kind of bottom he could imagine bouncing up and down naked on his hard cock, James had to turn away and stare out the window as he discreetly readjusted his trousers around the crotch area, *down boy down* he told himself, damn that woman was hot and she had no idea how she was making him feel.

As Annette returned after getting the drinks James was staring out of the window, he jumped when Annette approached 'sorry James' Annette laughed, you looked like you were in your own little world,

'Just thinking about work,' James could not meet Annette's eye's when he replied.

Annette sat down and sipped her drink, her top lip was moist and when she licked the wine off her lips James felt himself stirring again, he quickly took a gulp of his own drink, he quickly wished he had not, He did not wish Annette to think he was some kind of jack the lad who normally downed his drink in one.

'So your work? James?' Annette began.

'James? Earth calling James?' James then realised he had not been listening to a word she had said, he was thinking about her soft pink lips tightly wrapped around his cock.

'I was asking about your work' Annette began again.

'Sorry' said James I was miles away again wasn't I, he quickly replaced the thought of Annette's lips with one of his grandmother tutting in disgust at him.

'Not much to say about my work really, I buy properties, do them up and sell them on,'

'Just like they do at Carrington's I suppose then,'

'Yes just like Carrington's, talking of Carrington's, I need to....' but his sentence was cut short by a squeal from Annette who suddenly jumped up of the sofa.

'Oh silly me how clumsy' somehow Annette had managed to knock most of her drink on the table, thankfully only some had landed in her lap.

'At least it was not red wine you were drinking' James said to her.

'Oh my gosh I am so sorry' Annette's cheeks were burning with shame, that would teach her she had been staring at his lips wondering what it would be like to kiss them, they looked so warm and soft.

'I must go to the ladies and try to dry this off.'

'Good idea' said James in return, 'would you like another unless you're planning on sipping it up from the table of course.'

As he reached for the empty glass that was in Annette's hands their fingers brushed and Annette felt like an electric spark had travelled through her body, she excused herself once more and hurried off to the loo to dry and rescue her new trousers.

As Annette dried her trousers under the hand dryer, she decided to stop all fantasizing about him as if he would find someone like her attractive, she was probably way too old for him and for goodness sake she was a mother and she was still actually married. A shudder ran through her body at that thought, James was not interested that was all there was to it, but he sent you the flowers said a little voice in her head, he was just being nice, he fancies you, 'shut up' she said out loud to herself then quickly looked around thankfully she was on her own in the ladies, her trousers were almost dry, she checked her hair which was still looking great and took a deep breath and walked back to the table, where James was sitting. As she reached the table she noticed a bottle of champagne and two glasses.

'I could have sworn that's not what we were drinking a moment ago.'

'It's ok though isn't it?' queried James.

'Just a small one, I'm driving.'

'So am I' replied James 'don't worry I've thought about that, it's a Saturday night, no work in the morning, and I noticed a line of cabs outside the station, and if you're not willing to share this with me I am sure the people on the next table would be over the moon with a bottle of free champers. He laughed;

'You can't do that' said Annette once you start giving out free champagne everyone will want a bottle.

'So you will share it with me will you?'

'I don't know, I have my son at home and a babysitter, oh what the heck' she knew what Maddie would say if she'd told her she had turned down free champagne, she knew Maddie and Daniel would be fine until she got home, so what the heck as she watched James pour her a glass.

'Here's to us' James said holding up his glass.

'Yes to us' Annette giggled as they chinked glasses.

The conversation flowed, James had asked her about her son, Annette had told him about Daniel and Maddie in great detail, when she had got to Daniel's age; 'never' exclaimed James 'you can't have a son that age you really don't look old enough',

'Very funny Annette' replied 'I am 30 you know'

'No I mean it' said James 'I could have a child that age too then,'

'Why?' Annette enquired.

'I am the same age as you,'

Now it was Annette's turn to look disbelieving,

'No truly I am, I can even show you my driving licence which has my date of birth as proof if you wish'

'No that won't be necessary' laughed Annette 'I believe you, I just somehow thought you were younger than that'.

'I will take that as a compliment than.'

They both laughed as James re filled their glasses.

The evening went by quick, too quick as far as Annette was concerned, they had chatted about everything and anything. Annette was reassured that James had not run a mile when he found out she almost had a teenager as a son, the conversation had flowed and Annette was relaxed, James had made her laugh so much her face was beginning to hurt from laughing and smiling so much.

'Goodness is that the time' as she looked at her watch it was almost half eleven.

'Time flies when you're having fun, don't you agree?'

Annette had to agree even though her head was feeling a bit woozy from drinking champagne on an empty stomach.

'Have you eaten' enquired James 'there must be somewhere that does food round here, I am starving' he admitted.

'Actually so am I' confessed Annette.

'Come on grab your things lets go.'

'Go where? asked Annette 'nowhere will be open for eating at this time of night,'

'I know somewhere that is' after grabbing his jacket he held on to Annette's hand and he almost dragged her outside in haste. 'Where are we going?' she asked giggling now, 'You'll see' as he marched on. Annette laughed as they rounded the corner.

'Ta'da' James pronounced as he waved his hand in the vague direction of the burger van parked up at the side of the road just past the train station.

'I have not been to one of these in years,'

'Well now's your chance, what will you have,'

'Let me think, I will have a double cheese burger with bacon,'

'Great choice Madam, two double bacon and cheese burgers please my kind sir' James said to the burger van guy.

Annette giggled as the man looked at the both of them, he said nothing just shrugged his shoulders and got on with cooking.

They sat outside the cab station and ate their burger while waiting for their cab.

'Next time I will take you somewhere a bit better to eat,'

'Next time' Annette almost choked on her last mouthful of burger.

'Well that's if you don't mind being seen in public with me again that is,' said James.

'Of course I don't mind, I just thought, well never mind, it does not matter what I thought, I would love to come for dinner with you, thank you'.

'Done' said James,

'Done' agreed Annette.

They looked at each other and laughed once again.

They had agreed that they would share a cab, the driver would drop Annette off first and then the cab would take James home, they sat in the back of the cab and giggled like school children all the way to Annette's front door. Like a true gentleman James got out first and held the door open for Annette which made them both laugh again. 'Thank you for a great evening' Annette said to James.

'No thank you for a great evening' James replied as he reached over and kissed her lightly on her cheek.

It felt like his kiss was melting a hole in Annette's cheek, so she quickly turned and went up the path to her front door, she turned around and waved as he got back in the cab, Annette watched him drive off with his hand sticking out of the window waving back, she was glad it was dark as her face must have been the brightest red it had been all evening, she took a deep breath and let herself in the front door.

Daniel was fast asleep on the sofa, with the sofa throw wrapped around him, Maddie was watching some American game show on the TV, she jumped up as Annette walked in.

'Well' she whispered excitedly,

'Well what' giggled Annette,

'Judging by the time' said Maddie as she tapped her watch face 'and the big grin on your face' as she pointed at Annette's face, 'I'd say you had best tell me all about it.'

Annette and Maddie went into the kitchen and as Annette made the coffee she told Maddie all about her evening as they both sat around the kitchen table.

James had been smiling all the way back to his apartment, he had such a great evening and had such great company he thought, this evening was by far one of the best he'd had. James paid the cab man and told him to keep the change. Once he got into his apartment he sat down on his sofa and closed his eyes. When he opened them again he found it was 7.32am he decided he best go get his car back, they had shared one and a half bottles of champagne which worked out roughly five glasses each, they had given the other half bottle to a couple on the next table who looked like they could do with some cheering up. He had a quick shower, dressed in jeans and a sweatshirt; while waiting for a cab to take him to the car, he was thinking about Annette, her dimples, the way she laughed, how amazing her body looked in the trousers and laughed to himself as he remembered the shocked look on her face as she had spilt her drink, he loved the way her hair shimmered, he had remembered it from the first time they had met, that reminded him, Nathan's wedding was only a few weeks away and he wondered if he could invite Annette. He thanked the cab man and got in his car and drove away relieved to see that it was still in one piece after being neglected by him all night, abandoned in a cold dark car park.

Annette awoke around 10am with a dull but not too bad headache, they had been laughing and chatting so much she had not kept count of how much she had drunk but she knew it was not that much as she'd had worse hangovers than this, perhaps she should drink champagne more often, she wished she could afford too. Maddie and Daniel were both downstairs and Maddie was cooking up a big fry up by the time Annette got downstairs.

'Morning mum, how was your evening?'

'My evening went well Daniel thanks for asking, how was yours?'

'Oh mum it was great' enthused Daniel 'Maddie let me stay up late and we even had ice cream at 9pm Maddie's cool mum can she babysit me again, she is much better than gran and granddad when they babysit?'

'We will see' laughed Annette, 'anyone for a glass of orange juice' as she walked over to the fridge. Maddie gave Annette a lift to the station car park so Annette could pick up her own car, as Maddie pulled up Annette noticed the Aston was no long there, the fat bald headed bloke had probably been with the mistress for the evening after telling his wife he was working late, or he could of actually been working late she reasoned with herself. Maddie was going to pop into her shop for a while, she had some new designs she had thought of last night and she had wanted to get them started as soon as she could, so after saying goodbye and having one last giggle over last night's events Annette and Maddie went in their separate directions.

Chapter Eleven

Annette had been at work for the last two days and had heard nothing from James, she arrived at work on Wednesday morning settled down behind her desk and dealt with a couple of enquiries regarding apartments to rent, when another flower delivery van pulled up, and another large bunch of flowers being carefully carried towards the office main doors, they can't be for me again she thought to herself, 'Annette at the front desk' said the delivery man reading from his work sheet.

'That's me?' replied Annette,

'Sign here,' the delivery driver said offering over his handheld device.

'Thank you,' Annette answered as she took the device from him

'Someone's a lucky girl,' the driver remarked.

Annette blushed as she signed and handed back the handheld device, as the delivery driver left she reached over and plucked out the card that was nestled neatly in the bunch.

Proper meal, my treat, this Friday 8pm? The card read, followed by a mobile number. 'Oh my gosh' squealed Claire, who had just walked in late for work, 'Are they from the same person?'

'Uh Hu' nodded Annette,

'He really must like you; you're so lucky Annette,'

'Thank you.'

'Wait till the girls upstairs hear about this, they will all be green with envy' Claire said as she walked towards the lift, Annette felt herself blush and her body tingle with excitement, she grabbed her mobile from her bag and quickly text Maddie asking if she would be able to look after Daniel again on Friday evening.

The rest of the week passed quickly and Friday was going slow for Annette, it was lunch time so in preparation for tonight's meal out; Annette was hurrying towards town to buy a new outfit, she had already planned with Maddie to buy something from her shop and was heading there now, 'Annette' a voice called from behind her, she turned around and James was standing there looking really nice in a smart suit with tie and matching jacket,

'James,' Annette exclaimed, she tried to smooth down her hair with one hand which now was frizzy due to not having enough time to wash or smooth it down this morning, she was planning on spending a good hour on her hair this evening ready for this evenings meal. 'I'm just on my lunch break,'

'Well it was either that or you were skiving' laughed James,

'I would never dare to skive, I don't have the bottle for it, even when I was at school I could never do something like that, some of the girls I used to hang around with did that kind of thing, but I was too scared of getting caught' she thought of Maddie running off at school lunch breaks to have a quick ciggie and to meet with which ever boy she was seeing at the time and the memory made her smile.

'Are you sure you won't let me pick you up tonight? you are still ok for tonight aren't you?'

'No its ok, yes, no, I mean, yes I am ok for tonight and no I am sure I don't need picking up but thank you for the offer,'

'8pm at the restaurant it is then,'

'Yup 8pm, see you then James,'

'Bye Annette,'

'Bye.'

Annette checked her watch after James had departed, Shit she exclaimed under her breath, she had just 15mins left of her 45min lunch break.

'You're cutting it fine' remarked Maddie as Annette hurriedly pushed through the door of Maddie's shop.

'Yes I know I'm not going to have time to find anything now' moaned Annette.

'Good thing I have already selected a few items before you came in then' laughed Maddie.

'Oh really did you, thank you Maddie,'

'Now what do you think of these....'

It was 7.15 by the time Annette was finally ready, fitted black trousers with sequin detail around the waist and around the bottom hems, a pale pink cashmere top both from Maddie's clothing range of course, Annette's hair was piled up and pinned in place so only a few wisps hung gently around her face, she was also wearing a pair of black kitten heels, with a quick squirt of perfume, she was ready to go, her tummy was doing somersaults again but Maddie, who was looking after Daniel, assured her she looked great and almost had to march Annette to her front door and shove her out of it.

James was in a hurry, he had just received a phone call from Tom which had him flustered, the new building he was buying; the owners had received another offer and it was a higher offer than the one he had originally made, the house he had put the offer in for was an old house in need of a great deal of modernisation, it had six bedrooms and plenty of garden space, James's idea had been to convert the main house in to flats and build another set of flats in the property's gardens, but leaving enough garden space for a court yard to enable the residents of his flats to have ample parking space and a still leave a little bit of greenery to sit in if they so wished, he felt it much more pleasing to the eye to have a bit of garden than just to have a big concrete parking lot, he had a lot to think about, but was now running late for Annette, he quickly showered and put back on the trousers he had worn but managed to find a clean and ironed shirt, thank goodness for the laundry service he used, it was his own fault about the trousers as he had not bothered to sort any out for cleaning, a quick blast of aftershave, a handful of gel and he was out the door, he did not have time to call a cab as Tom had called just as he was about to do so, so he had to take the car, damn no drinking for me tonight he muttered to himself as he wheel spun the car out of his garage and headed towards to town to meet Annette.

Annette had been standing outside the restaurant for the last ten minutes, she kept checking her watch, then checking her phone, no texts, no phone call, what if he'd realised he did not actually want to meet her but did not have the nerve to tell her, what if he had found out about Simon and thought he should stay well clear of damaged goods. Don't be silly she told herself, he could not of found out about Simon, only her parents, Maddie and of course Daniel knew and they would not of said anything, but what if one of them had done, stop it! She told her head firmly they would not of done anything like that to me perhaps he is just running late, she checked her watch another ten minutes had past, he was now twenty minutes late, she could feel her eyes begin to water and her shoulders slumped, she pulled her phone out her bag and was going to call Maddie, she turned away from the restaurant and began to walk back to where she had park her car.

'Annette!' 'Annette!'

She turned and laughed when she saw James running up the road towards her, he almost collided with a poor man who had just left the wine bar further down the road, he was smiling and waving wildly at her, and her stomach began to do somersaults again.

'Please forgive me Annette, I am so sorry, I truly am, I had a blooming phone call about work, then I could not find a parking space so I had to park in the station car park again'.

'Well if you were on time,' Annette replied with a smile on her face 'you would have found plenty of spaces in the car park behind here' as she gestured towards the restaurant.

'Plenty of spaces you say,'

'Yes plenty,' 'well two or three free places perhaps,'

'Hummm' was all James replied grinning at her, which made her somersaults turn in to backflips, large backflips.

'Let's eat I'm starving, said James he her held her gently by the arm and led her into the restaurant.

James had asked for a quiet corner when he had phoned to make the reservation 'of course' had come the reply when he had told them his name, 'you may sit anywhere you wish young James' this was the same restaurant his parents had eaten in regularly when he had been growing up and were on first name terms with the owner and most of the staff, 'how are your delightful parents still enjoying sunny Cyprus?'

'Yes Mr Dhawan my parents are both fine, thank you,'

'It will be a pleasure to see you again.'

As promised, James and Annette had been seated at a table near the window away from the doors, as to avoid any disturbance to them when other diners were leaving or entering.

The food was delicious, Annette had enjoyed every mouthful, she had asked James if he thought the chef would give her the recipe for the chicken tikki masala and they had both laughed when James had replied 'yes, but he would probably have to kill you after'. Annette had ordered Gulab Jamun with vanilla ice cream for dessert and James had ordered a coffee, he knew he was running out of time to ask her, but every time he tried, the words failed him, he took a deep breath and tried again, 'Annette, would you mind, I mean would you come, will you....' he stopped talking when he realised Annette was starting to laugh at him.

'Spit it out' she laughed,

James took a quick swig off his coffee and managed an 'Ouch!' as the steaming hot coffee burnt his mouth, Annette was looking quizzically at him now, 'it can't be that bad,' she said with a serious tone in her voice,

'No, no' repeated James 'it's not bad, it's just, well, I wanted to ask you to accompany me to my friend's wedding in a couple of weeks time.'

'Pardon' was all Annette said as she was managing not to choke on the spoonful of ice cream she had just eaten.

'My friend's wedding, will you come?' James tried again.

Annette put down her spoon and looked at James trying to work out if he was serious or if it was some kind of wind up, her heart was beating wildly in her chest, he looks serious Annette thought, he was staring at her now, waiting for an answer, 'oh my gosh, you really are serious,'

'Sorry perhaps I should not of asked you, it's just, well, I really like you and we have been having so much fun, I just thought it would have been nice if you came with me and meet my friends, well my closest friend my best friend,' James began to realise he was rambling so just ended up shrugging his shoulders and took another more careful sip of his coffee this time, he kept his eyes fixed to his coffee cup, which made Annette laugh again as his eyes crossed over when he took another sip of hot coffee.

'Sorry' muttered James beneath his breath, 'I just thought' Annette interrupted James 'Thank you for your offer and providing I can get my parents or Maddie to look after Daniel, I would love to come with you.'

'Oh you would, that would be great,' enthused James as his eyes met hers, she felt all hot and flustered, oh how his eyes twinkled she thought, and he stood up, pushed his chair back, reached over and gave Annette a gentle kiss on her lips, Annette felt herself go bright red from head to toe, her lips tingled and other parts of her body began to throb wanting more. They finished at the restaurant and after a struggle with who was paying the bill, it was finally agreed that James would pay for this meal and Annette could pay for their next.

'Oh my gosh,' squealed Annette when she arrived home to Maddie,

'Where is Daniel' Annette then said in a hushed voice,

'He's asleep, so tell me everything' Maddie whispered back.

Annette ushered Maddie in to the front room carefully shut the door behind her, she squealed again as she turned to

Maddie, 'He has asked me to go to a wedding with him, his best friend's wedding, and he said he really likes me' Annette gushed out in one heavy breath. Maddie reached out and hugged Annette.

'Did you say yes?' 'Are you going?' 'Oh my God Annette I am so happy for you' Annette and Maddie then both began to squeal with excitement,

'Just one thing' Annette said as they both finally stopped squealing,

'What's that?'

'I have not asked my parents to have Daniel yet,'

'I am sure they will say yes, and if they don't I can always have him again,' said Maddie.

'Oh would you really,'

'Of course I would,'

And they both began squealing again.

Chapter Twelve

Annette's week had past rather quickly, she had seen James a couple of times at work but he was always rushing past with Tom, they had spoken on the phone a couple of times and had been texting each other. James was busy until the date of the wedding which was fine with Annette, her and Maddie had been busy themselves, Maddie had insisted on making a new outfit for Annette, so their free time had been filled with measuring Annette in all the right places; colour planning, not to mention matching shoes, Maddie had been working into the small hours, cutting and sewing material in her boutique. Annette was due in tomorrow which was the Saturday before the wedding. Her parents had said they did not mind having Daniel at all and had offered to have him Friday night until Sunday evening; Annette tried to tell them this was not needed but they insisted and told Annette she could have the whole weekend to relax and enjoy herself.

Seven days till the wedding, it was now Saturday and Annette was heading to Maddie's boutique for a fitting, she was excited as Maddie had kept most of the design quiet, but they had agreed on five different colours.

Annette had reached Maddie's, Julie was at the till and looked up and smiled at Annette as the bell above the shop door signalled Annette's arrival, 'she's outback if you want to go through' Julie said to Annette.

'Thank you Julie I'm so excited, what colour is it?'

Julie laughed, 'she won't let me anywhere near it, I am dying to see it myself but not till you've seen it first, as I keep getting reminded.'

Annette walked through the shop, she passed the changing rooms and through a door marked 'Private, enter at your own risk', Annette knocked gently on the door, 'Maddie, it's me' she called,

'Just a minute' came a muffled response.

Annette waited all of thirty seconds 'has it been a minute yet?'

Annette could hear Maddie laughing from the other side of the door,

'Please Maddie; you have made me wait a week already,'

'Okay, count to ten, and then you can come in,'

'1, 2, 3, 4, 5, 6, 7, 8, 9, 10' Annette counted as quickly as she could and opened the door,

In front of Annette stood Maddie, her hair was all over the place and she had material covering every surface in the room, all sorts of colours and all types of materials. Annette had never been out back before, she was amazed at how big the space was, there was even a sofa, TV and a little kitchenette tucked away in the far corner, but most of the space was filled with mannequins, some in half states of undress, some just wearing a hat. Most were wearing items of clothing you would class as a working progress. Two mannequins, the two that Maddie was standing beside, were fully clothed, one was wearing the most stunning dress Annette had ever seen; the dress was black, with the most delicate copper beaded detail around the neck line, complimented by small copper beaded flowers. The second outfit was a trouser suit, pale pink halter neck top with a lilac pattern across the top of it and the trousers were the same pink with the same lilac pattern around the hem and waist band.

'What do you think' grinned, Maddie.

'I think, Gosh!' 'Are those really for me?'

'Yup both yours, the trouser suit for the wedding and the dress for evening reception' said Maddie still grinning.

'Oh Maddie, they are stunning, they really are wonderful, I don't quite know what to say, thank you, thank you so, so much' she walked over to Maddie and gave her a big hug.

Chapter Thirteen

On Monday, Annette awoke feeling lousy, she'd had a restless night's sleep, filled with dreams about dresses ripping, falling over in new shoes, six days until the wedding; Annette wondered if it would be too late to ring James and cancel. Annette's phone beeped just as she was getting out of the shower, it was from Maddie asking Annette to pop by for another dress fitting, 'oh,' sighed Annette it was too late to cancel, James's feelings aside, Maddie had gone to all that trouble in making the outfits for the wedding and evening reception. Annette could not let her down. 'Looks like I am going then' Annette said out loud to herself, 'going where mum' Daniel shouted from his bedroom, 'nowhere, get out of bed and get ready for school, breakfast in five' As she went downstairs she heard the shuffling of feet and the light switch getting turned on from Daniel's bedroom, 'oh no!' Annette groaned as she walked into the kitchen and noticed Daniel's school uniform still in a heap on the floor next to the washing machine, 'Mum! Where's my uniform?' Daniel shouted out from the bathroom, 'bollocks!' muttered Annette under her breath she had been so preoccupied with other things going on she had completely forgotten to wash it; it's partly Daniel's fault as he had only brought it downstairs yesterday evening while Annette was on the phone to her mother, who was worried about Frank, who had spent most of the afternoon hugging the toilet while retching. After Annette had finished on the phone it was gone 10pm and Annette had just gone to bed without remembering to put the wash on overnight. Annette grabbed Daniel's stuff and shoved it on a quick rinse and spin whilst getting breakfast ready. Daniel came downstairs still wet from the shower, 'oh *mum*' he whinged, 'please don't tell me that's my uniform spinning around in there?' pointing at the washing machine, 'sorry darling, I completely forgot, I had nanny on the phone, granddad sounded really poorly from what she was saying; he was throwing up all afternoon and you know what granddad gets like, he is hardly ever ill.'

'Other than that time in Corfu' they both said at once and laughed.

Corfu was where Annette's mum and dad had gone on honeymoon and Frank had ended up ill for most of it and Josephine never tired of telling them the story of how she spent her wedding night listening to the sounds of the, then, new husband Frank being sick all night after getting food poisoning from a meal one of his lady friends had cooked him a week before the wedding.

By the time Annette had got to work she was 10 minutes late; she screeched the car into a parking place, grabbed her handbag and burst through the office doors. She was hot and flustered and really not expecting what she saw. James and Tom were standing in front of her desk deep in conversation; they both looked up when she came flying in. Tom looked at Annette in shock and when James looked at her a faint smile appeared on his lips, 'Sorry Tom' Annette said breathlessly trying to avoid eye contact with James, she felt herself flush from head to toe, 'is everyone alright Annette?' enquired Tom. 'Yes everything is fine, had a slight hiccup at home this morning.'

'I trust it won't happen again,'

'No sir, Tom, it won't happen again sorry,' Annette blushed again *oh my gosh I called him Sir how blooming stupid am I.*

She tried to avoid James's eye but as she looked up he was still looking at her and the faint smile was now a bigger smile which made Annette blush even more, as she stumbled over her handbag, to get to her desk, which she had left on the floor. James took Tom by the arm and steered him towards the door; as they walked away Annette overheard James saying to Tom 'don't be too hard on her Tom, everyone is entitled to an off day.'

'Yes well I suppose your right' agreed Tom.

And with that James turned around and gave Annette a wink which sent a delicious shiver down her spine.

Work! Annette, think about work she told herself as she watched Tom and James walk towards the car park, she could not help but notice James had such a tight and pert looking backside, she wondered what it would be like to run her hands over it. Work! She told herself again.

At lunch time Annette checked her phone and turned it off silent *1 new message* the small screen in her hand read,

Hope you're ok and it was just a minor case of the hiccups.

Annette grabbed her handbag and headed off to the bakery on the High Street for a bite to eat while texting a reply,

Just a panic over school uniform, thanks for asking.

Annette had just reached the bakery when her phone bleeped again,

It did not look like you were wearing school uniform from where I was standing ;-)

Annette laughed out loud as she read that one, then felt herself blush as she realised a few other people had turned around to look at where the laugh had come from. Annette coughed slightly and text back.

I don't think I could still fit into my school uniform, if I tried.

Bleep went her phone before she'd even had a chance to put it back in her pocket.

You must send me a picture if you do ever try and don't wear it to work you may give poor old Tom a heart attack.

Cheeky, I would have thought it would make Tom ill rather than give him a heart attack and I think I might just get the sack there and then if I did. Annette text back to that one.

After buying her sandwich, chicken, lettuce and mayo on crusty white bread, she hurried back to work to eat it in her car, she did not want to be late back to work after lunch; late twice in one day would not look good.

I doubt that very much, replied James.

She finished her lunch in record time and after putting her phone back on silent she went back into work. By the time Annette had finished work she was shattered, she just wanted to pick up Daniel, have a nice hot bath and a large glass of chilled white wine. Daniel had gone to his friend's house for tea after school instead of Annette's parents as her dad was ill. A couple of bits of cheese on toast for dinner would do her after picking up Daniel followed by her bath and glass of wine.

As she put her cheese on toast under the grill she quickly walked into the front room and pressed play on the answer phone.

'Hiya luv it's me' Maddie's voice Annette knew at once, 'I did try your mobile a couple of times but it just rang, this message is just to remind you final dress fitting on Wednesday after work if your mum can hold on to Daniel a bit longer that normal'. Oh gosh thought Annette, Wednesday, three days till the wedding and her stomach did a little flip.

'Hello love, it's your mum here' started the next message, why do mother's always say it's your mother calling, like after all these years we had not learnt to recognise their voices by now, 'Really sorry' continued Josie her mother 'we won't be able to have Daniel again tomorrow, your father's really quite bad he has spent most of today in the bathroom, it's coming out both ends of him now if you know what I mean, will call you again later, bye love.'

Yuck! Thanks mum I know exactly what you mean thought Annette as she pressed delete on the answer phone.

BEEP BEEP BEEP BEEP.....

'Oh bloody hell' exclaimed Annette out loud as she hurried into the kitchen turning off the cooker in passing to open the kitchen window, grabbed the tea towel off the side and started flapping furiously at the smoke alarm.

'Dinner's ready then mum' came Daniel's voice from the hallway as he walked in passed her, reached up and pressed the button on the smoke alarm; the noise stopped immediately. Now Daniel was eleven he was almost as tall as his mother 'dinner?' Enquired Daniel as he peered over his mother's shoulder and took in the sight of the charred remains that was Annette's cheese on toast. 'Never mind, nanny put me off eating anyway' Annette muttered to him.

As Annette laid in the bath, the wedding was going around in her head, why did she say yes to James, why would anyone go to wedding of someone they don't know, never mind that; I don't even know James that well, what on earth was I thinking I must cancel, you can't cancel; remember, three days to go for a start and you can't let Maddie down with the dress fitting, that reminds me, 'Daniel' Annette called from the bathroom as she was getting out of the bath, 'you're going to have to be at home till I come back from work by yourself tomorrow, granddad is still ill, do you mind?'

'It's going to cost you' replied Daniel cheekily as she walked from the bathroom and in to her bedroom.

'Hummm I thought it might' 'another new computer game by any chance,'

'Arrrr yer mum that would be great, thanks for the offer; I was just going to say can you leave me some money for a pizza delivery.'

Annette laughed as she pulled on her pyjamas 'I will see what I can do, night love,' she said as she turned off her light and got into bed,'

'Night mum, Mum?'

'Yes love,'

'Thanks.'

Chapter Fourteen

Annette was in work early again today; she was in early yesterday as well to make up for Monday's fiasco. Today was Wednesday, final dress fitting day which meant three days to go, the nerves were getting to Annette now, she was not too sure what she was actually nervous about, was it seeing James and again? Was it going to a wedding?, Not just any wedding though, James was best man and Annette would not know anyone else there at all. What if people assumed she was James's girlfriend or partner, what would she tell them, would she say "we're just friends," or "we work together," perhaps this last statement was not 100% true but they did work in the same building every now and again. When Annette actually thought about it, she realised she did not know exactly what James did other than he shows Tom a few buildings he may be interested in; maybe he is actually a surveyor or an architect thought Annette. She checked her watch, it was almost 5pm, nearly time to go and have her final dress fitting. She really wanted to leave dead on five today and get straight to Maddie's shop, she had a quick phone call to her during her lunch break but that was not enough, she really needed Maddie to reassure her that everything would be ok, that by attending this wedding with James she would not be making a huge mistake. Part of her was excited about seeing James again and spending more time with him, a whole weekend she thought, I must ask him about hotels and where we are staying; James had text her at the beginning of the week to say that the hotel was booked. Annette had never asked if they had separate rooms or if he had booked just the one room for them both. Oh no she thought to herself what if he expects me to sleep with him! I really should have booked the hotel myself. She also remembered he had not actually let her know how much the hotel room had cost so she did not know how much to pay him back. Annette rechecked her watch 5pm on the dot; she packed up her stuff and left the building at 5.01pm, 5.15pm she flew into Maddie's boutique, 'Afternoon Julie' Annette said as she walked in the shop, 'Afternoon Annette, she is waiting for you out back just go through.'

'Thanks Julie' Annette replied whilst not stopping, and continuing to walk out back, 'Maddie where are you?' 'This is going to be a disaster.'

'What's going to be a disaster' said Maddie as she appeared from the far end of the back office space,

'Everything' moaned Annette.

Maddie laughed 'don't be silly, you're going to have a great time.'

'What if he has booked us into the same hotel room, what if he expects me to sleep with him in the same bed, what if he wants to have sex!, oh my gosh Maddie what am I going to do?'

Maddie tried not to laugh but the look of panic on Annette's face was quite funny.

'Just sit down will you and have a cup of tea or something, you're making me dizzy watching you pacing up and down in this room.'

'Sorry Maddie, I just don't know what I was thinking when I agreed to go.'

'You're going and will have a great time, and if he tries anything on you can always knee him in the bollocks and run.'

'Run to where' continued Annette 'I will be stuck in the middle of nowhere with him and all his friends and no car' Annette sat down and held her head in her hands.

'Ok then' you kick him in the nuts, run, hide somewhere and call me and I will drive straight down and rescue you, or you could get a train or you could lock yourself in your hotel room until I rescue you, or you could fly to the moon and back.'

Annette looked up with a confused look on her face 'fly to the moon and back?'

'Just checking you were still listening to me, you're just getting worked up over nothing, you might go away and have the perfect weekend, and if you don't then at least you were wearing the best outfits.' Maddie walked over and gave Annette a big hug,

'Yup, you're right I'm worrying over nothing aren't I,'

'Yup afraid so,'

Annette stood up and hugged Maddie back 'you're such a great friend what would I ever do without you,'

'You would be wearing shop bought clothes without me, that's what you would be doing' laughed Maddie.

'Now let's get the clothes sorted, I can't have you looking almost perfect, it's my name on the line you know.'

They both laughed as Annette tried on the outfits once more; Maddie pinned and sewed the last few bits that needed doing until the outfits were actually perfect.

It was gone 8pm by the time they had finished 'Wow' breathed Annette when Maddie finally let her see herself in the mirror, 'they really are perfect, thank you ever so much Maddie, really, thank you, thank you, thank you.

'I will bring them around Friday evening after work so you will have them ready to pack Saturday morning, some of us poor single women don't have the ability to be whisked off for a weekend away by a gorgeous, young man.

The two friends' laughed as they packed the clothes away and hung them up on Maddie's finished rack. They turned off the lights and made their separate ways home.

'Sorry I was so long' Annette said as she let herself in through her front door.

'Daniel' she said a bit louder as she got no response, she walked towards the front room door where she thought she could hear Daniel talking to someone, 'Daniel' she said again only this time her voice was a bit shaky, it was quite an unsure voice that spoke his name. As she reached out and turned the door handle to the front room she held her breath not knowing who or what was going to be on the other side.

As she walked in the front room she noticed the TV was on.

'Ok bye' she turned to where Daniel was sitting and let out the breath she had been holding, 'Don't ever do that to me again,'

'Do what mum? Are you ok mum? You have gone really pale.'

'I heard you talking, I thought' then Annette shook her head 'it doesn't matter darling' she was not about to tell Daniel what she had been thinking, the words I thought your dad had found us, echoed around in her head as Daniel told his mum all about the girl whom he had been on the phone with.

Chapter Fifteen

Beep, Beep, Beep, went Annette's alarm, Annette rolled over and thumped it quiet, *Aaaaargh one day to go* was Annette's first thought, she groaned and pulled the pillow over her head.

'Hello, mum, it's me, sorry to call so early I was just checking how dad is and to see if your still ok to have Daniel this weekend?'

'Oh hiya luv, I was just getting out of bed,'

'Its 8 am mum, are you ok? I thought you were normally up at seven?'

'I know luv, your dad's still not too good, the sickness seems to have stopped but he was tossing and turning and kept waking me up on and off all night,'

'Does that mean you won't be able to have Daniel now?

'Of course we can still have Daniel love, even if I have to banish your father to the bedroom all weekend, having Daniel is still fine, so don't you worry about that.'

'Only if you're sure mum, I could always cancel going to the wedding you know,'

'Don't be silly, you go the wedding and have a great time - no need for cancelling,'

'Ok mum as long as you're sure,'

'Of course I am sure; we will have a great weekend together.'

'Ok then mum, right I need to go, really don't want to be late for work,'

'Ok love, we will see you and Daniel tonight.'

'Yes mum, see you tonight, love you.'

'You too love, bye.'

'Bye mum.'

Damn! Annette thought as she put down the phone, that would have been the perfect reason not to have been able to go, oh well looks like I have to go now whether I like it or not. Her tummy did a perfect back flip at the thought of spending a whole weekend with James, a whole weekend with James her mind told her for a second time, 'Shut up!'

she scolded herself but at the same time a slight grin appeared on her face.

On the way to work she called Maddie, 'how do you fancy, pizza, movies and a few glasses of wine tonight,'

'Oh', 'I don't know' 'Let me check my diary' Maddie paused as if she really was checking her diary, 'You are very lucky, I happen to have a space free, right after I drop some of my gorgeous clothes to a gorgeous client of mine who happens to be going for a wicked weekend away with the man of her dreams.'

'I am not sure about the man' laughed Maddie 'but the bit about the clothes is right,'

'See you at seven then.'

'Yes see you at seven', 'Oh and Annette?'

'Yes'

'Everything will be fine.'

'Are, you, su...'

'Yes I *am* sure' cut off Maddie; 'now get into work before you lose your job.'

'How did you know I was not already at work?' asked Annette looking around in case Maddie was close by.

'I could hear you drumming your fingers on the steering wheel.'

'Ok, okay,' laughed Annette and stopped drumming her fingers.

'See you tonight.'

'Yup see you tonight' replied Maddie with what Annette could only describe as a sing song voice.

At lunch time, Annette finally plucked up the courage to text James, *Are you sure you still want me to come with you?*

Yes, why, are you getting cold feet? came the quick reply.

No of course not, lied Annette.

Good, 9 am tomorrow it is then.

Yup, tomorrow 9 am.

Annette's phone rang, 'Hello.'

'Hello.'

'James?'

'Yes, it's me. I think you are forgetting to tell me something.'

'Am I?' replied Annette slightly confused.

Shit! Thought Annette he's found out about Simon and he thinks I am still married oh bollocks what am I going to say, what to say, think quick, shit, shit, and shit! Annette took a deep breath and was about to explain all to James when he laughed and said 'I need your address.'

'Oh gosh, how stupid of me!' Annette breathed out a huge but silent sigh of relief and told him her address, finished the phone call and her lunch and went back into work to finish the rest of the day.

She gave Daniel a quick bite to eat and was running around straightening up the house; it did not actually need doing but every time she stood still she could not help but think she was mad for going away with James and she did not want to be thinking about it now, anyway it's too late she told herself firmly you are going and that is that.

'Mum? Daniel's asked,

'Yes love, Annette said whilst getting out the Hoover to clean, an already vacuumed floor.

'What's this man like, you're going away with?'

Annette stopped what she was doing with the Hoover,

'Well' began Annette sitting down opposite her son at the kitchen table, 'he is a very nice man, he makes me laugh, he's kind, and he buys me flowers' she said while using her arm to gesture across to the kitchen window where another superb display of flowers sat in their vase. Annette had just finished work and was grabbing her handbag when a flustered delivery guy walked in holding a gorgeous bunch of flowers:

'Delivery for Annette' he announced breathlessly.

'Oh, that's me.'

'Sign here love.'

'You ok? enquired Annette looking at the delivery man's flushed face.

'I am now.'

Annette looked at the delivery driver with a confused look.

'Rush order, me love, the call only came in an hour ago for these, said he would pay me double if I got them to you before 5 pm, correct me if I am wrong, but it is 5pm on the dot' he said looking at his watch.

Annette looked at her own watch, indeed it was 5pm. 'Thanks.'

'No thank you, that's the quickest one hundred quid I ever earnt.'

'One hundred pounds!' gasped Annette as the delivery driver walked off.

'He must have done something really wrong or you've done something really right' he winked at Annette as he walked out of the office doors.

Annette blushed and reached inside the flowers for the card.

Can't wait till tomorrow, don't worry., x

Read the card, damn was it that obvious I was nervous Annette thought.

'Mum you're grinning, what are you thinking about?'

'Nothing,' blushed Annette.

'Oh no you're not in love with him are you mum?'

'Don't be silly Daniel I have only known him a few months.'

'Now let's get your stuff together and get you to nanny and granddad's.

'You could have let Maddie babysit.'

'She has to work my darling, now you finish your tea.'

Daniel nodded.

'Right, grab your stuff and we will be off' she said to Daniel's retreating back,'

'Yes mum' he said as he turned around,

'You will always be my number one man, you know that don't you Daniel?'

'Yes mum and you will always be my number one mum.'

They both laughed as Annette opened her arms and enveloped Daniel into a big hug.

Chapter Sixteen

Annette had tried to relax, but instead she was pacing up and down her hallway with a large glass of wine in her hand. Maddie had text to say she would be late as something had come up that she needed to work on for one of her private clients. Like she did for Annette, she designed one off items of clothing for her wealthier clients, the kind of clients who liked a new outfit for every different occasion and they paid well for it. Annette had guessed that one of these clients had appeared suddenly and wanted Maddie to whip up a new outfit for her, and wanted it for the weekend.

Annette had taken Daniel to her mum's, 'Hi love' Annette's mother said when she had opened the front door.

'Hiya mum' Annette had replied giving her mother a kiss on both cheeks, 'how's dad' Annette asked when they were inside and her mum had shut the front door.

'Your dad's fine, he's in the front room waiting for you both, do you want a cup of tea love?'

'Yes please mum that would be great.'

'Daniel?'

'No thanks gran, I am fine, can I plug my Xbox in and play with granddad please?'

'You will have to ask your granddad that one but I am sure he will say yes.'

'Have you beaten my high score yet son?' said Frank from the front room.

'You wished it was your high score' replied Daniel opening the sitting room door with his Xbox and games in his hands.

'You come in the kitchen with me love, you look like you could do with a sit down.'

'Let me just say hi to dad then I will be through.'

'Ok love.'

Annette walked into the front room and kissed her dad on his cheek as she sat down beside him.

'You feeling ok now dad?' enquired Annette.

'Of course I am love, you know me.'

'I can always cancel going if you're not up to looking after him dad,'

'Don't be silly love, we will be fine, wont we Dan?'

'What's that' said Daniel who was plugging leads from the TV to the games console and vice versa,

'I was just saying to your mum here, that we will have a great weekend won't we boy,'

'Yer of course we will, you have all weekend to beat my high score now' he said to Frank as he passed him over one of the controllers.

'As long as you are sure dad.'

'Yes love its fine.'

Annette sighed and got up to join her mum in the kitchen, as she walked out of the room Daniel and her dad were deep in conversation about the latest level Daniel had completed.

'Here love' her mum said passing her a cup of tea.

'Why do I get the feeling you're trying to get out of going to this wedding?'

'Oh mum' Annette sighed.

'It's not that, well I suppose it is partly, I just don't know if I am doing the right thing by going, I have not known him that long and what if no one else there likes me.'

'I am sure everyone there will like you love and I know you have only known him a few months but what the heck, you deserve to have some fun in your life you know.'

Annette took a gulp of her tea 'do you really think I am doing the right thing going?'

'Well you will never know until you go, will you love? You don't really want to be sitting at home wondering what it would have been like if you had not gone do you?'

'I suppose your right mum; I'm just worrying over nothing.'

Annette put her tea down on the table and walked back to the front room where she could hear Daniel jokingly calling his granddad a cheat, and the sound of her father laughing in response; quietly Annette shut the front room door and walked back into the kitchen and sat back down.

'I am going to divorce Simon, mum' Annette blurted out.

'About time too,' came her mother's response. Annette looked at her mum with a shocked expression on her face.

'What did you expect me to say, no dear stay with the nasty, horrible wife beating man?

'Well no, but, I, I don't actually know what I expected you to say, but I don't think I was quite prepared for that response.'

'Sorry if that shocked you love, but I can never forgive him for what he did to you, me and your dad trusted that man to take care of you and look after you and look how he treated you.'

To Annette's surprise her mother had tears in her eyes.

'Oh mum, don't get upset.'

'Sorry love it's just sometimes me and your dad both get so cross when we think how he treated you and we really regret not coming to visit sooner, but when you said how busy you all were up there we felt it was wrong to push ourselves on you to visit.' Josie wiped her eyes with the corner of her kitchen apron she always wore over her clothes when cooking or cleaning.

'Oh mum I am so sorry.' Annette reached over and hugged her mother over the table.

'It was my fault mum, not yours, I lied to you. I lied to everyone; I never wanted anyone to know what a mess I had made of my life and I kept on thinking he would change. He was not always like that you know mum, but he just slowly turned into this kind of monster and the drinking got more and more and the behaviour got worse and worse, then he had the affair and then you turned up with dad and I finally realised that enough was enough. I did not even really think about what I was doing that day, I just knew I had to get away and I had to get Daniel away. What kind of life would we have both had, if I had stayed any longer?' Annette shuddered at that thought, 'but now I am away from all that and that part of my life is over, once the divorce comes though then that part of my life would be over and done with for good, please don't get upset mum, please.'

'I'm sorry love but you know you and Daniel mean the world to me.'

Annette checked the time on the kitchen clock, 8.07pm the clock read. 'Oh gosh mum I did not realise it was so late, Maddie will be at mine soon if she is not already there, I really must get going, you ok now?'

'I am fine now love' her mum said getting up front the table and giving Annette a big hug 'you go and have the best weekend ever with your new man.'

'Mum, he's not my new man.'

'Well he should be, I can't wait to meet him, sounds delicious.'

'Mum! He's a man not a piece chocolate!' laughed Annette.

Annette went and gave Daniel a big hug goodbye. She made him promise to be good and gave her dad a hug goodbye. At the front door her mum gave her a small box in her hand, 'just a little something for tomorrow my love.'

'Mum you shouldn't have.'

'But I did, so now it's too late, take it and off you go in case poor Maddie is sitting on your doorstep.' Annette opened the box. Inside was a small pair of diamond earrings, 'but mum' began Annette, 'They were mine love, your dad gave them to me a few years ago but I have never worn them; you will get more use out of them than I will, you can wear them tomorrow.'

'Oh, thank you mum' Annette said, giving her mum one last hug before tucking the box in her handbag and getting into the car; she waved goodbye to her mum and Daniel who were both standing on the door step waving, 'bye' Annette called out of the window as she drove off home.

Chapter Seventeen

'Wakey wakey, sleepy head' came Maddie's sing song voice as she sat down on Annette's bed, 'rise and shine big day today.'

'What time is it' asked Annette rubbing her eyes and trying to sit up.

'6.30am,'

'Oh Maddie, my alarm was set for 7.00 am,'

'Yes well, that's not long enough for you to have breakfast, get showered, dressed and have your hair curled now does it?'

'*My* hair curled?'

'Yes *your* hair curled, now drink your tea and eat your toast. I will make sure everything is ready to be packed, what shoes are you going to wear?'

'Oh help!' exclaimed Annette as she put her cup of tea down on the bedside table next to her now cold, soggy toast,

'What am I going to do with no shoes' she wailed as she lay back on the pillow and threw the duvet over her head.

'Wait there' ordered Maddie.

'What, under the covers?'

Annette waited for a reply from Maddie but when none came she took the covers off her head to find Maddie had gone from the bedroom. Annette got out of bed and wrapped herself in the dressing gown that hung from the back of her bedroom door, 'Maddie, Maddie! Where have you gone?'

'Stay there I will be back in a minute' came Maddie's voice from downstairs.

Annette could hear Maddie thumping around downstairs and sat back down on her bed to finish her tea.

Maddie walked back into Annette's bedroom with both her hands behind her back.

'What have you done now?' Annette sighed and turned to face her best friend who was grinning from ear to ear.

'Ta, da' Maddie announced as she produced a pair of black shoes from behind her back.

'Oh Maddie' Annette exclaimed as she took the shoes from Maddie's outstretched arms 'where, how?'

'I made them.'

'You made them.'

'Well actually they are yours.'

'They are *mine*?'

'Well kind of, they are your shoes but I just added the pattern on to them.'

'But how?'

'I stole them from you.'

'You *stole* them from me!?'

As Annette looked at the shoes, they did look familiar to her, but Maddie had added tiny copper coloured beads in the shape of a flower stuck onto the front of the otherwise plain black shoes; the beaded flowers matched perfectly with the beaded flowers on Annette's dress, Maddie was explaining how she had gone through Annette's wardrobe looking for shoes to go with the outfit when she was babysitting Daniel the last time she was at Annette's and had found the shoes shoved right at the back of the wardrobe gathering dust.

'I knew you would not notice they had been missing' laughed Maddie.

'I had forgotten I had them.'

'I thought as much judging by the thin layer of dust that I had to wipe off before putting the beads on.'

'They are perfect, thanks Maddie.'

'No probs hun, what are friends for now come on you, it's time for your shower and hair curling.'

'Yes mum' saluted Annette as both the girls laughed.

By 8.30 am Annette was standing in front of her full length mirror in her hallway downstairs by the front door looking at herself, stunned by her reflection. She looked at Maddie whose reflection was standing behind her in the mirror and Maddie had a huge grin of satisfaction on her face as Annette looked from Maddie to herself in the mirror. She was lost for words, the person she was looking at looked nothing like she did yesterday and looked far from the person who had woken up at 6.30 am this morning.

Annette's hair was curled around her face, long, dark, soft, bouncy, shining curls, the kind of curls you see on TV adverts and on the heads of catwalk models, certainly not what you would expect to see on Annette Johnson aged 30 and single mother of one. Maddie had dressed Annette in a pair of tight but comfy black tailored trousers and a navy blue fitted lightweight jacket, Annette had a white strappy top under the jacket and on her feet she wore a pair of low healed navy blue ankle boots that they had both found hidden in the back of Annette's wardrobe, along with a pair of bright pink high heeled shoes that Annette had bought last year as they were the bargain price of five pounds.

Maddie had done Annette's make up perfectly, it was a plain look that made Annette look like she was not wearing any make up at all, A brush of bronzer over her cheekbones made her look like she had a healthy glow to her cheeks and her eyes had a quick flash of mascara and a soft smudge of eyeliner on the bottom lashes, a soft pale pink lipstick gave Annette's lips a hint of colour and brought out the fullness of them.

'How am I ever going to thank you for all of this?'

'No need for thanks the look on your face says it all, just call me your fairy Godmother.'

'I am not sure Daniel would actually like having a fairy as a Godmother.'

'I can be your fairy Godmother and his plain old boring Godmother.'

'You are not boring, Daniel loves it when you have him for me and spoil him rotten like you do.'

'Well have I have been his Godmother since he was four months old on that freezing cold January day in the church.'

'Oh I feel so old now, he's eleven years old!'

'You're not old; you're the same age as me.'

'Yup like I said, Old!' and as they both started laughing the sound of a car engine pulling up outside Annette's house made them both stop suddenly and they held their breath as they heard a car door open and shut.'

'Oh my gosh it's him' said Annette, her heart was pounding in her chest.

'Go and get your stuff from upstairs, I will open the door for you, quick before he knocks.'

Annette ran up the stairs two at a time and grabbed her bag, she had packed a couple of changes of clothes for Sunday, her pyjamas, towels and toiletries, the black shoes, wrapped in tissue paper were on top of everything else, along with a pair of bright pink shoes to match the trouser suit, a pair of flat black shoes; the dress and trouser suit from Maddie were hanging in their suit covers over the wardrobe door to avoid getting dirty or creased on the journey. Annette reached up and unhooked them from the door as she heard her doorbell chime, oh my gosh, its him, its him, it's really him, sang a voice in her head, dear God, if you're out there, please, please don't let him turn out to be nutter she said silently while looking up towards the ceiling. Annette could hear voices from the front door, Maddie was talking to him, but they were talking so quietly Annette could not make out anything that was said. Annette took one last deep breath to try and control her nerves and walked down the stairs carrying her bag and the outfits from Maddie.

'Hi' Annette said shyly from the bottom of the stairs.

'Hi' replied James.

'Let me take them for you' and as he reached over and took the bag and clothes from Annette his hand brushed against hers and sent a tingle of excitement all through her body.

'His car' mouthed Maddie,

Annette shook her head as Maddie gestured towards the road, where James was putting Annette's bag and outfits carefully in the boot of a small silver car.

'What is it' whispered Annette to Maddie 'is it a bad car?'

Maddie pulled Annette into a hug and whispered into Annette's ear, 'just don't press any buttons.'

'What?' Annette whispered back not quite understanding what Maddie was getting at.

Annette never had time to hear Maddie's reply as James was back in front of the door asking if Annette had got everything.

'Yes I think I have' answered Annette moving away from Maddie towards the car 'Oh no, hold on' said Annette as she dashed back inside and ran upstairs; she went in to her bedroom and into her bedside drawers and pulled out the small box containing the diamond earrings her mum had given her last night and went back downstairs.

'Almost forgot them' she said to both James and Maddie showing them the content of the small box.

'Do you want me to put them in for you now?' offered Maddie.

'No that's ok I will put them in once I am changed and ready for the wedding.'

'Ok' said Maddie 'have a great time' whilst pulling Annette into another hug.

'Nice to meet you Maddie' said James offering his hand for Maddie to shake.

'Nice to meet you too' Maddie took his hand and shook it.

'Nice arse' Maddie commented to Annette, with a wink as James walked back to the car.

'Shush' said Annette as she nudged Maddie.

'You are right though' she told Maddie as they both watched James get into the car and shut the driver's door.

'Go and have a great weekend' said Maddie giving her dearest friend another hug.

'I will, hopefully.' Annette crossed her fingers and walked to the car and felt silly - the car, it was the same car she had seen in the car park the night she met James. Oh well she thought, at least this car's owner is not at all like I imagined. One more quick hug with Maddie and Annette was climbing into the passenger side of the car. With Annette and James in the car, seat belts both on and Maddie waving from Annette's front door, they pulled out into the road and started the journey to Hertfordshire.

Chapter Eighteen

The roads were clear and the sky was blue, James's car was something else, thought Annette as they drove through the town towards the motorway; the journey was roughly an hour and fifteen minutes away - so far the only thing James had asked her was 'are you ok?' to which Annette had replied 'yes thanks, you?' followed by 'yes I am fine too.'

Annette was starting to wonder if she could tell James to turn around and take her home, to also tell him what a big mistake this had all been, but she decided she could not do such a thing, adding to the fact they had just hit the motorway.

Now was probably not a good time to tell him anyway she thought.

James broke the silence! 'Would you like some music on?'

'Why not, but how do you work the radio, there are so many buttons in this car; do you actually know what they are all for?'

'The radio button is top right, next to that is the CD button and these buttons down here are my secret weapons' said

James as he gestured down next to his handbrake between them both.

Annette reached out and turned the radio on, 'what do you want to listen to?' she asked the car was filled with the sound of classical music. 'I never had you down as a classical kind of guy,'

'Why not' laughed James 'I am not really I was stuck in a traffic jam yesterday and I was trying anything to calm me down,'

'Did it work?'

'No not really' confessed James and they both laughed, in the end they agreed to settle on a station that was playing a mixture of music some 80's, some 90's and some up to date stuff.

Annette was still looking around the car. 'What's that button do?' she asked while pointing at a button on the top of the dash in front of her, 'try it' replied James so Annette pressed the button and gave a small shriek of shock as the glove box sprung open on to her lap, 'why did you not warn me that would happen' she demanded of James, 'where would the fun have been if I had told you.' was James's cool response, Annette laughed and playfully slapped him on the arm; as she pulled her arm away from his, James caught it and held her hand over the handbrake. Annette blushed but did not move her hand away as she felt the electricity that had been building in the car since their journey had started pass between them. Annette felt more relaxed and sank back into the posh leather seats and closed her eyes for a few seconds.

When she opened them again James quickly looked away. 'Two eyes on the road Mr Harrington' Annette exclaimed in mock horror. James let go of her hand and put both hands back on the steering wheel, 'about that' he began 'what does this button do?' Annette said over the top of him and before he'd had a chance to reply she had pressed it and let out a loud shriek as the roof of the car started to fold back. 'Oh my gosh, stop it, stop it' demanded Annette as she was trying to stop her hair from flying around in the now open topped car. James looked at Annette and laughed 'you pressed it' he said 'yes but I did not know it would do that, did I?'

'You should have waited for an answer then before you pressed it' James shouted in response.

'Okay, okay, you're right, now how do I close it before my hair is completely ruined not to mention my make up!'

'You press the button again,'

'Pardon,'

'I said, you press the button again' James pressed the button this time as the roof started to close them back in the car once more. James stole a sideways glance at Annette who was still holding down her hair with both hands, James turned back to face the road as a big grin appeared on his face; after the doubts he had had, he finally realised that this weekend was going to be a great weekend and he knew Nathan, Kathleen and everyone else were going to like Annette. 'It's not funny' Annette said noticing James had a big grin on his face 'no of course it's not, sorry' yet the grin on his face grew wider.

The rest of the journey was filled with talking, laughter and the music playing in the background.' James had offered to stop at the services in case Annette needed a bathroom stop to sort her hair before they arrived at the hotel; they only had around twenty miles left to go. Annette declined but did use her fingers and the vanity mirror to restore some kind of order to her hair, which in fact did not look that bad after all, thankfully from where Annette had held down her hair during the roof incident not much was out of place. It was not as perfect as it was when Maddie had finished it but it was still far better than anything she could have done. After going around the third roundabout in a row, they turned right, then left and then Annette noticed the hotel; it was not just a hotel but a large leisure complex, 'wow' breathed Annette as they drove up the driveway to the building, which dated back to the 1800's as James had told her when she remarked how beautiful it was. James went on to tell her about the people who once lived here and about an 18th century man whom the house was apparently named after.

It was 10.17 am by the time they had parked the car in the courtyard of the building.

'What kind of place is this, you can't tell me it's just a hotel it's huge.'

James laughed' did you not read the large sign welcoming us as we turned up the drive.'

'No, I was too busy looking at the building itself,'

'It's a luxury resort,'

'What else do they have here?'

'Golf, spas, gyms, tennis, swimming pools and I believe they even have a nature walk.'

'Have you been here before?' enquired Annette,

'Once or twice,' replied James.

Annette turned and longingly looked at James, without saying anything she thought he must have read her mind. She felt her womanly urges appear; the tingling within, the racing of her heart beat, she wanted him: Snap out of it Annette you are not a lustful youngster anymore! she thought. It had felt like she had been stuck in a time warp ogling, lusting over what stood before her when James said that he and Nathan sometimes met up here and to have a few rounds of golf, Annette just nodded.

'So what do you want to do first?' James broke the silence.

Jump into bed and shag your brains out Annette thought but turned to James and shrugged her shoulders, not daring to open her mouth in case the words she had just thought tumbled out.

'Well I thought you might want to do something as we have three and a bit hours left until the wedding.'

'Oh, I am not sure,' said Annette 'I would not mind going for a walk in the grounds if that's ok with you.'

'Yes of course that's ok, now let's get our things up to our rooms and we can work it out from there.'

Annette nodded again and got out of the car, she was relieved to hear that James had used the word rooms when talking about taking their stuff inside and had not used the word room.

She was relieved but also excited about the feelings she had just opened herself up to again, it had been so long. Annette had forgotten about sex, the way being that close to a man had made her feel. Simon was a good lover when they had first met. She really had a good appetite for him in the beginning, could she imagine herself in the closeness of another man again?

Chapter Nineteen

Annette and James had both checked in and to Annette's relief they were given two separate keys to two separate rooms in fact their rooms were on different floors completely. They had agreed to meet back downstairs in Reception in half hour. Annette walked down the corridor to her room, she was fishing around in her handbag for her mobile so she could call Maddie as soon as she got in the room; as Annette walked inside the room she was amazed, the room was huge and across two separate levels. As she walked from one level to the other she noticed in the middle of the room was a four poster bed; as she sat on the bed clutching her mobile, she noticed she also had her own dressing table; she left her phone on the bed and walked around the huge room. There was a bar full of tiny little bottles, and a coffee table with a lovely fresh bunch of pink and white roses and magazines, as she picked one up to flick through she noticed that they were this week's editions, unlike when sitting at a doctor's surgery the magazines are dog eared and at least a couple of years old. Along with the mini drinks there was your normal tea and coffee and chocolate chip cookies which were delicious thought Annette as she took a bite.

She even had her own private garden space. The bathroom looked like it had never been used and she even had a towelling bathrobe all folded and neatly wrapped in tissue paper on the side; the bathroom had lots of little bottles of things including, shampoo, conditioner, bubble bath, body scrub, moisturisers, make up remover and more. Annette really wished Maddie was here to see it all, 'shit Maddie' Annette thought and hurried from the bathroom through the 'living area' and down a couple of steps to the bedroom where she'd left her mobile on the bed.

Annette was just finishing her conversation to Maddie when she heard a faint knock on the door, 'oh gosh' how long have we been on the phone?' 'about half hour' said Maddie 'oh gosh, that will be James at the door I was meant to have met him, twenty minutes ago!' gasped Annette as she checked the time on her watch, 'I best go,'

'Don't do anything I wouldn't do' came Maddie's sing song voice.

'Shut up' hissed Annette into the phone 'I will call you later.'

'You had better; I don't want to be calling the local police station demanding they dig up the whole place to find your body.'

'That's not funny; I will call you later I promise, bye.'

'Byeeeeeeeeee' came Maddie's sing song voice again as Annette pressed end call.

'Oh I am so sorry' said Annette when she opened the door to find James standing there 'I lost all track of time.'

'That's ok' replied James 'I just wanted to check you had not got lost, I can come back later if you're not ready or we can just meet up at 1.30pm to go straight to the church if you want?'

'No, no, I am ready, let me just grab my handbag, come in.'

'Thank you' said James as he walked in and shut the door behind him.

Annette walked into the bedroom while holding in her tummy and trying to wiggle her bum subtlety, but sexily; then she felt silly so she just walked a bit quicker away from James and grabbed her handbag. When she walked back into the room, James was standing by her garden area, 'is it the same as yours?'

'I don't have a garden at home' and after seeing the confused look on Annette's face he smiled the sexy smile that made Annette's inside somersault yet again.

'I don't have a garden off my room; I thought you might have liked it.'

'What do you mean you thought I may have liked it, did you have something to do with me getting this gorgeous room?'

Annette looked at James's face and noticed he had suddenly gone a bit flushed.

'James! Please don't tell me you booked this room for me especially.'

'Do you just want a reply or the truth?'

'The truth, please James, from the start.'

James took a deep breath 'ok, yes, I had something to do with this room.' Annette looked at him stony faced and raised her eyebrows at him. 'Ok, ok I had everything to do with this room, I booked it, I paid and I even asked for those flowers to be put on the coffee table.'

'James! When I asked you about the room you said everything was taken care of, I did not expect you to pay, I could have paid for it myself you know.'

'But you did not have to, I wanted to treat you and I know you would have argued with me if I said I was going to pay. So when I said the rooms were sorted I meant it.'

'I thought you meant the bride and groom had paid for it.'

'Well they did offer, but I said I did not mind, you even got an upgrade from the rooms they were booking.' James smiled that smile again; Annette was so cross with him for deceiving her but when he smiled, her whole body lit up, how could she be cross with him, when he was so damn sexy.

'Please forgive me Annette' James walked over and took both her hands in his. 'I am sorry, I won't do anything like that again.' James leaned in and his lips brushed hers; electricity rushed through Annette's body and she ached for him, he kissed her again, slightly harder on her lips this time - she felt his soft tongue tease the outside of her lips. She then thought if she dies now she would die very happy; she kissed him back, their tongues entwining around each others. James' hands were around her waist pulling her closer into him. When they finally broke apart James's green eyes were staring into her own, she could feel his warm breath on her face. She wanted him and she wanted him now, then she remembered her son. 'Right,' she finally said and taking a step back from James, he dropped his arms, she grabbed her handbag from the floor where she had dropped it at some point during the kiss, grabbed James's hand and pulled him towards the door. 'Sod the walk - I need a drink!' she marched out of the room still holding James's hand and only stopping to shut the door behind them as they headed down to the bar still hand in hand.

Chapter Twenty

Annette was laughing, James had just told her the story of how him and Nathan had met and how he was the geek in the glasses and how Nathan had come to his rescue and they had been best friends ever since. He also explained that he and Kathleen had never really got on, but they did their best for Nathan. James did not go on to explain that he had been to bed with a couple of her friends, including one of her close friends who was a bridesmaid. When they had been attending the dress rehearsals, he had seen her and managed to pretend that nothing had happened between them but every time James had glanced up at something the vicar had said he had caught her staring at him, so he just smiled and turned away. The last thing he wanted to do was either start an argument or have her thinking he was still interested. 'Oh my gosh, James!' Annette suddenly exclaimed 'it's 1pm. The wedding starts in an hour. We need to get ready.'

'Is it really 1pm already? Doesn't time fly when you are having fun' and there it was again, that grin. Annette could picture all her inside turning to mush and she had to steady herself on the bar as she got down from the stool where she had been sitting. They both quickly drank what was left in their glasses, Annette's was a now warm glass of white wine and James's was an equally now warm coke, 'meet you by the main doors in half hour, ok?'

'Ok' agreed Annette, James pulled her close and gave her another kiss, his lips on hers were soft and sent a tingle down her spine, it was soft and slow no tongues this time but the kiss was equally as good as the last kiss they had shared. Annette giggled like a school girl and then blushed at the giggle she had just let out, quickly she turned and headed back to her room before she dragged James with her and they never made it to the wedding at all. She got her outfit from the wardrobe where she had hung it, while she had been talking to Maddie earlier, she had no time for a bath or shower and she did not want to ruin the makeup Maddie had done so well on earlier that morning; she touched up the makeup and added a fresh coat of lipstick and a squirt of her perfume. A small piece of paper had fluttered to the floor, when she had taken the clothes off the hanger; she bent down to pick it up off the floor and looked at it: *you will be fine, go get him tiger grrrr*, the note read, *luv Maddie x x x*. Annette laughed to herself and took one last look in the full length mirror, the suit fitted her perfectly and the makeup was still looking great, despite kisses and roofless cars. She took a photo of herself and sent it to Maddie, is it still too late to back out! Annette had added under the photo. While she had been getting ready she had managed to make a quick phone call to her parents, to make sure Daniel was behaving, which he insisted he was; her mother had told her not to worry, this was her weekend away and told her to enjoy it. 'How is the delightful James today anyway' her mother asked.

'Mother!' hissed Annette 'I hope Daniel never heard you say that.'

'Of course not, luv, he's back in the front room with granddad, ready to beat him again at that computer game they have been playing all day.'

'I told you not to let Daniel play it that much.'

'It's not my fault luv, your father keeps getting Daniel to play. I think he's determined to beat him even if he has to stay up all night,' her mother laughed and so did Annette.

'Ok mum, love you.'

'And we love you too dear, very much.'

Annette checked her phone one more time before turning it off and putting it in her bag, Maddie had still not replied.

Annette reached the main doors; James was already standing outside with another man, who was wearing an identical suit to James. Annette was filled with nerves as she took a deep breath and approached them both.

She was nervous about how she looked, nervous about meeting Nathan, nervous about the wedding; in fact she was just nervous about everything.

James took a step towards her and kissed her on the cheek, 'you look good enough to eat' he whispered in her ear, he gave her a wink and turned around to introduce her to Nathan. 'Sorry I never joined you both for a drink earlier, I am so nervous I would have drunk the bar dry and been curled up on the floor sound asleep by now and I never would have made it to my own wedding.' They shook hands as Annette replied 'You look great,' and without thinking she reached out and straightened up Nathan's tie.

'Oh my gosh, I am so sorry.'

'Don't be, I was never any good at doing ties.'

'I tried to tell him it was wonky but he would not believe me' added in James.

'Was it really wonky?' Nathan asked Annette.

Annette blushed slightly and nodded 'just a little bit.'

'See I told you' teased James, taking Annette's hand in his own.

'Ready?' James asked Nathan.

'Ready' replied Nathan.

'Let's do this' they both said in unison as the three of them made their way to the waiting wedding car.

Chapter Twenty One

James had done his bit perfectly and Kathleen looked beautiful, in an off the shoulder cream ruffled bodice, with matching ruffled dress and a long train, with two bridesmaids walking behind, her wearing soft lilac dresses that matched both James and Nathan's shirts perfectly. Annette at one point had noticed the bridesmaid on the left giving James the eye, a kind of flirty look with a come and get me grin; Annette was not going to let it bother her. God knows she has a past of her own and she was not going to let anything or anyone in James's past spoil what they had now. Annette could not help but think if she was that bridesmaid she would have done the exact same thing to James herself. The suit he was wearing was dark grey and fitted his body to perfection, the lilac shirt brought out the colour of his eyes, his lovely, twinkly green eyes.

Annette had felt slightly awkward at first sitting at the end of the front row with Nathan's parents next to her. Annette was sitting next to Nathan's mother; James had introduced her as his partner and squeezed Annette's hand as if to confirm it. He looked at Annette when he said it and she did not disagree. When they had sat down, James was standing at the altar next to a still very nervous looking Nathan.

Nathan's mother had leaned over to Annette and said 'I am so glad we finally got to meet the only woman who could be responsible for the remarkable change in James. We thought the day would never come when he met a nice woman like you, to finally sort him out.' Annette was dying to ask what she meant by all that, but the organist had started playing and everyone was facing the doors waiting for Kathleen to enter.

Annette was a bit shocked when Nathan's mother grabbed her hand and squeezed it during the 'I do' bits; she did not mind as at the same time she had squeezed James's hand without taking her eyes of the bride and groom; let's hope your marriage is better than how mine turned out, she thought as James passed her a tissue to dry the tears. Annette had not known she was crying.

James had been watching Annette on and off for the whole service; he loved her singing voice and the way she did not shake off Nathan's mother when she had grabbed her hand as he looked back at Nathan and Kathleen just married. To his surprise, he pictured himself and Annette standing at the altar and Annette wearing a stunning wedding dress, he tried to shake the picture from his mind as the music started up once more for the bride and groom to make their way outside. He smiled to himself as the picture slowly faded from his mind but as he smiled to himself, he knew from the moment he had seen Annette in the night club almost eight months ago now, that she was the one for him, he never wanted to lose her and he felt his heart skip a beat when that thought had entered his head. He just hoped and prayed that Annette felt the same way about him as he felt about her; he took her hand as they stood up and followed the newlyweds out of the church for the next hour of photos that followed.

Annette had tried to protest when James and Nathan agreed she should be in the wedding photos herself and she could really not say no after Kathleen had encouraged her to do so herself. Annette stood next to James with his arm tightly around her waist, while they all posed and yelled *happy, happy, happy* as the camera man had insisted while he took the photos. Annette thought the bridesmaid had given her a dirty look at one point between photos, but then Annette suggested to herself it could have just been a squint the bridesmaid had, due to the sun being so bright and not a dirty look at all. Yes, agreed Annette to herself, in her head, it must have been a squint after all, as she and James made their way to Nathan's parents' car, who were giving them both a lift back to the hotel resort. With James's hand tightly in hers she did not care about anything or anyone else right at that moment, the only thing she cared about right now were the feelings of happiness that were bubbling away inside her.

Chapter Twenty Two

On the drive back to the hotel resort, with James and Annette sitting in the back of Nathan's parents car, Annette was sure she kept on seeing Nathan's mother using the vanity mirror to have a quick glance at them both while on the pretence of checking her hair and makeup; James was chatting both to Nathan's parents and to Annette, Annette was so glad she had not chickened out of going, today was turning out to be one of the best days Annette had spent in a long time. She had liked all the other people she had met and Nathan's parents were keeping Annette entertained with stories relating to James' and Nathan's childhoods. Annette was also learning bits and pieces about James's parents and had realised that she had never asked any questions regarding his parent's whereabouts. So far she had learnt that James's parents were living abroad, retired from working in a development company; so that's where James must have got his know how from, to be working for Carrington's. What a shame, Annette thought, that James's parents had retired as he could have carried on working with them and perhaps James would have been working for Harrington's rather than Carrington's. On the other hand she was quite relieved James was not actually working for his own parents as it might have ended up with James being her boss! How horrible would that have been, the old cliché of sleeping with the boss sprang to mind. Annette shuddered at the thought. 'Are you cold' enquired James, damn thought Annette he must have felt the shudder. 'No, not really;' she could not really tell him she was shuddering at the thought of James being her boss. 'Oh come here.' He put his arm around Annette and pulled her closer into him. As Annette snuggled into him she noticed Nathan's mother having another quick hair or make up check in the mirror, but this time as she looked at Annette she could have sworn Nathan's mother gave her a slight wink! They still had a couple of hours until the reception and evening entertainment consisting of a buffet for 250 people. As they drove back up the driveway towards the resort Annette was still snuggled into James and right there and then she wished the car journey to the hotel would never end; when they reached the car park Annette had to tear herself away from James's shoulder and James turned to her and said 'Quick drink? Then I will leave you in peace to get ready?' 'Yes that sounds great.'

'Thank you Mr and Mrs Filtz-Fenton,' Annette said to Nathan's parents when they all got out of the car as she shook their hands goodbye. Nathan's mother moved closer to Annette and still holding her hand said quietly to Annette: 'Call us Bob and Patricia.'

As she moved closer she whispered to Annette 'After all dear, I am sure we will be seeing a lot more of you from now on' and gave Annette another one of her winks. 'Yes, I am sure we will; after all we will both be at the reception tonight, yes dear, just you wait and see,' and with that Patricia turned around linked her arm through her husband's and walked into the hotel.

'What did she just say to you?' asked James in a hushed tone, 'you look a bit confused.'

'Nothing much.'

'To the bar then?'

'Yes, take me to the bar' laughed Annette.

It was now 5pm, Annette and James had finished their drink at the bar and Annette was now sitting on the lovely comfy bed, waiting for the bath to fill, whilst dialling her mother's number.

'Hi mum it's me' said Annette when her mother answered the phone.

'Hello love, how did it go, did they both turn up?'

'Mother! Of course they both turned up.'

'Shame' laughed her mum, 'I do love a bit of gossip every now and again; how was it, did the bride look stunning?'

'How is that lovely man of yours?'

'Yes, the bride did look stunning and he is not my man mother.'

'Don't tell me he is still just your "friend" Annette.'

'Yes, no. I mean yes he is still my friend, but he is not *my man*, he is his *own man*, not *just* mine.'

'Not just your man, I hope you're not having one of these open relationships.'

'No mother it's not like that.'

'Either he is your man or his not then.'

'Ok, ok mum then he is my man if you want to put it like that.'

'Oh goody,' said her mother and Annette could picture her mother sitting down at the kitchen table with a big grin on her face, and that's just what her mother was doing.

'Now that's out of the way, would you like you speak to Daniel?'

'Yes please mum and don't go telling Daniel, I want to tell him myself in my own time please mum.'

'That's fine with me; invite him in for tea when he brings you back won't you love.'

'I will think about it, but no promises mum.'

'Ok love, I will pass you on to Daniel.'

Annette walked into the bathroom and turned off the taps while her mother called Daniel into the kitchen. They did not have one of the new fangled walkabout telephones; they had tried it once but Annette's father Frank was always losing them or forgetting to put them on charge, so they had the one that plugged into the phone socket in the kitchen and one upstairs in the bedroom. Annette had guessed her mum had answered the one in the kitchen as she could hear the washing machine spinning in the background.

'Mum?'

'Hello sweetheart, how are you? Missing you'.

'Missing you too mum. Granddad is getting really good at the console games, he has actually beaten me!'

'Granddad has managed to beat you? How long have you actually been playing the console today?'

'Not that long. Nanny made us turn it off for lunch and we must have it off again for dinner in a moment. Nanny said we could play on it again tomorrow. That is ok, isn't it mum - to play again tomorrow?'

'Of course it is, but don't think I will be upping your game playing time when I get home.'

'Oh mum.'

'Oh mum nothing. You know the rules!'

'Yes mum. Can I go now before granddad cheats and I only have twenty minutes left till nanny said dinner was ready.'

'Ok darling, I will let you go, say hi to granddad for me and I will see you tomorrow afternoon.'

'Ok mum.'

'Actually Daniel, I need to ask you a grown up question before I go. Would you mind if James came in for a cup of tea when he brings me home tomorrow?'

'Will he bring me a present?'

'I doubt that very much Daniel.'

'Aw not fair, but I suppose that would be ok, now can I get back to my game please mum?'

'Ok sweetheart, love you and miss you.'

'Love you and miss you too mum, bye.'

'Bye sweetheart.'

Chapter Twenty Three

Annette had a nice long soak in the bath and had tried not to get her hair or make up wet, which was a difficult task in itself, but she still did not want to ruin either. She had phoned Maddie straight after her bath and was still wrapped in the towelling dressing gown that was every bit as warm, soft and fluffy as it had looked in the wrapping. She had given Maddie the full run down and Maddie had whooped with delight when Annette told her they were officially seeing each other, "Go girl" had been Maddie's exact words which had made Annette blush and a warm feeling run over her body at the same time. Annette said goodbye after promising to give every single detail of this evening's do to Maddie in the morning.

Annette slipped into the black dress and looked at herself in the mirror; it really was the best dress Annette had ever worn and the shoes matched even more perfectly than they had when Annette had tried them on at home. It was now half past six, half an hour until the reception was starting and again she was meeting James at the main bar in Reception. Annette had a last look in the mirror, grabbed her handbag and headed down to the bar. As before, James was sitting there, but this time he was talking to a woman;

Annette felt a stab of jealousy as she saw the woman laughing at something funny James had just said. Annette did not like the way the woman; or the bridesmaid as Annette recognised who it was, flicked her hair and batted her eyelids, so fast Annette thought her lashes might fall off. The bridesmaid looked at Annette as James turned around; 'Wow, even more delicious, than when I saw you earlier.' Annette blushed, as again she caught the same look the bridesmaid had given her earlier. It was a dirty look! Thought Annette to herself. The cheek of it!

'See you later then, shall I?' said the bridesmaid to James.

'Yup whatever.' James dismissively said back, as he walked towards to Annette and took his hands in hers.

'Do a twirl for me' James asked Annette as the bridesmaid walked off towards the banqueting hall, where Nathan and Kathleen were having the wedding reception.

'A twirl? what? here? now?'

'Yes a twirl here and now, let me' said James as he held one of Annette's hands above them both and pirouetted Annette in a full circle.

'Come here sexy' James growled to Annette as he pulled her into his arms for a hug 'If you were not with me already,

I would make damn sure that by the end of tonight you would have been.' Annette giggled 'What makes you think I would have wanted to be with you?' She laughed and hugged him back and they walked hand in hand into the wedding reception.

The room was lit up by candles on the tables, the band were playing some kind of soft ballad as people were arriving. James was still holding Annette's hand as he walked around the room saying hello to different people and introducing Annette as his partner. It still gave a warm glow to Annette to hear him calling her his partner; the buffet was lined up against the far end of the wall and the tables were set out around the outside of the dance floor space, a few couples were on the dance floor and a few people were already seated at their tables. The tables had everyone's name places written on cream card with gold writing. As Annette was being introduced to another couple both James and Nathan had known from their school days Annette glanced at the buffet; it was the most impressive buffet Annette had ever seen, there was not a sausage roll or pineapple and cheese on sticks in sight; it was all little bits of cheese on little bits of what looked like crackers, pâté on small triangles of bread or toast. Annette was a bit disappointed about the lack of pineapple and cheese on sticks and the sausage rolls, as they were her two favourite things to eat at parties. Kathleen's father walked onto the stage to the right of the buffet table and announced that the bride and groom would shortly be arriving and asked if everyone could take their seats. Annette and James found themselves at the head table, along with Nathan and Kathleen's parents. Annette was seated in between Nathan's mother and James which she was quite pleased about, as she had met so many people over the last twenty four hours she really did not want to have to remember anyone else's names and besides, she liked Nathan's mother.

The bride and groom finally made their grand entrance and the whole room stood up and applauded them both.
The speeches were now in full flow; Kathleen's father had done his and James was half way through his, retelling a tale from their school days of how Nathan and Kathleen had met, when Annette felt someone staring at her. In the dimly lit room she looked around, everyone was looking at James and laughing in all the right places; Annette finally spotted who was staring at her, it was the bridesmaid. What's her problem? thought Annette as James sat down and grabbed Annette's hand, his speech was finished. 'Was I ok?' James leaned over and whispered in Annette's ear. 'Of course you were, it was the best speech I have ever heard,' which was kind of true as Annette had only her wedding reception to compare too, and well, we all know how that turned out.

Annette shuddered at the thought of Simon; she really must tell James, but not tonight, here and now was not the place to be telling him something like that. The champagne was flowing, the bride and groom had their first dance, the buffet table was open and people were already loading their plates with all sorts of mini goodies. James had gone to get them both something to eat, Nathan's parents were already on the dance floor; Annette watched as Nathan's father twirled his wife on the dance floor. Nathan and Kathleen were locked in each other's arms swaying in time to the band. Annette jumped as someone appeared beside her, 'Oh you gave me a fright' she exclaimed. 'He was mine first and don't you forget it bitch' spat an angry voice. Annette looked up at the speaker and her mouth fell open in shock as the words registered in Annette's mind. 'But, what, who?' was all Annette managed to stammer as the bridesmaid turned and walked into the sea of people on the dance floor. 'You ok?' asked James with a frown as he returned to the table with two platefuls of food, 'You look like you've just seen a ghost?'

'Yes I am fine, must have just had a dizzy spell or something. What kind of food is it?' asked Annette desperate to change the subject.

Chapter Twenty Four

Annette had picked at some of the food and had excused herself from the reception by telling James she had a bad headache and needed to lie down for a bit. James had wanted to come with her but Annette had assured him she would be fine in a bit, and would join him again later when the headache had eased a bit. The truth was she was a bit shaken up after what the bridesmaid had said to her, no one had ever spoken to Annette like that, other than Simon but he did not count, she got up to her room, sat on the bed, pulled out her mobile and called Maddie.

'What's wrong?' Was the first thing Maddie said as she answered her phone.

'Nothing, I was just calling to see how you were.'

'Don't lie to me Annette, what's the bastard done to you? I swear if he has laid a finger on you I will come down and hurt him.'

'Calm down Maddie, it's not him, he has been perfect. It's just…'

'Just what Annette, I am getting my shoes on to come and rescue you.'

'No Maddie I don't need rescuing, it's just…'

Annette went on to explain to Maddie all about the dirty looks from the bridesmaid and what the horrible cow had said.

'You ok now?' asked Maddie as the conversation came to a close, they had been talking for an hour and Annette felt a lot better.

'Yes thank you Maddie, thank you so much.'

'You know what you got to do?.'

'Yup, I know thanks again.'

'Go for it girl, love ya.'

'Love ya too, bye Maddie.'

'Bye.'

Annette put the phone down, touched up her make up in the bathroom mirror, took a deep breath and walked boldly back downstairs to the wedding reception. As Annette entered the room almost everyone was on the dance floor, she could not see James at first, then she spotted him and her heart sank, he was on the dance floor with that cow draped over him, he was saying something to her and he did not look that happy Annette was pleased to see. She remembered what Maddie said and took another deep breath and marched towards James and *the cow*; once she reached them, she saw the look of horror register on *the cow's* face and a big grin appeared on James face. 'My man, my dance I believe.' said Annette as she elbowed *the cow* out of her way and out of James's arms. James wrapped both his arms around Annette.

'Oh I am yours now, am I?' said James in mock horror 'how you feeling?' he asked as he kissed her softly on her forehead.

'Better than I have in a long time' said Annette and she meant it. James was hers and she had never felt surer of anything in her life. She did not even notice *the cow* had left the dance floor; *the cow* hurried out to the toilet with tears brimming in her eyes. *The cow* had never lost a man in her life, even if he was someone else's that had never stopped her before. What did that bitch have that she did not; she remembered trying to push herself into James and grind with him, James's words rung in her head, 'stop trying' he'd said. 'I know what you're trying to do, I have found the most perfect woman and not even a *bitch* like you is going to ruin that,' and then *that bitch* turned back up and elbowed her out of the way. What did *that bitch* have that she did not, thought *the cow* sadly to herself as she sat on the cold hard loo seat and dried her tears. She always had the man she wanted, no matter if he was someone else's or not, that had *never* stopped her or them before, until now!

Before long the wedding reception was finally over and everyone had waved goodbye to Nathan and Kathleen as they left to start their honeymoon, two weeks in the Caribbean no less. James was walking Annette back to her room hand in hand both giggling as the champagne took hold, 'Goodnight' James said as they reached Annette's bedroom door 'Goodnight.' Annette giggled back. James leaned forward and their lips met, it was a slow passionate kiss that left Annette wanting more as they pulled away from each other, 'Thank you for a wonderful evening' said Annette. 'No, thank you for the most wonderful evening;' Annette giggled again, head light with champagne and the kiss, her body was aching for more than just champagne as James kissed her again, harder than before but soft and sensual, his tongue probing in Annette's mouth, Annette's tongue wrapping itself around James tongue, as they pulled away, Annette was going to ask James to come in. 'Good night Annette, see you in the morning.' James kissed her on the forehead and turned to walk away as Annette put her key in the lock to unlock the door. 'James' Annette said as she managed to get the door open, her heart beating wildly 'Yes' as he turned around and looked at Annette, she took in his green eyes, his toned and tanned body, she longed to run her hand down that chest to feel his strong arms wrapped around her naked body. 'Goodnight James' was all Annette managed and as she walked in the room and closed the door. Damn she thought to herself, 'Goodnight James' she mimicked herself saying, as she got undressed and slipped into bed. She was too cross with herself to even bother taking off her make up! 'Goodnight James' she mimicked to herself once more before falling fast asleep.

James had gone back to his room and had helped himself to a miniature bottle of brandy from the mini bar in his room; as he sat on the bed and sipped it he scolded himself, what's wrong with you man, you know she was gagging for it, she was a bit drunk he told himself, it would not have been fair, she was not that drunk, he responded to himself, that's never stopped you before; now look at you, a solid hard one and nothing to use it on. Oh shut up! he told himself as he finished the brandy in one shot, got undressed and got into bed, it was an impressive hard one he consoled himself, just a shame she never got to see it, James sighed; turned off the light ignoring his throbbing cock and went to sleep.

Chapter Twenty Five

The journey home was a strange one, they were both talking and still enjoying each other's company but there was this electric energy in the air and every time Annette looked at James she imagined pouncing on him there and then in the car and shagging him senseless. Annette was wearing a skirt and shirt and looked stunning again thought James. He was picturing himself sliding his hand up her skirt and rubbing the inside of her leg, feeling the warmth of her thighs on his hand before slipping his fingers inside her knickers, playing with her until she moaned and demanded he stopped the car and shagged her senseless, if she was *actually* wearing knickers that was. With that last thought, he really felt a large bulge start to form in his trousers and he had to think of his grandmother again, which made him shudder in disgust but at least it had stopped himself growing too hard under his trousers.

'Would you mind dropping me off at my parent's house?' Annette's voice broke through James thoughts.

'No of course not but you will have to tell me how to get there.'

'That's fine, but I must warn you my parents are expecting you to come in for a cup of tea, but you can always say no if you're busy.'

'No, that would be nice; I don't mind meeting your parents.'

'It's not just my parents that will be there,' Annette took a deep breath 'my son will be there too.'

'That's still ok with me, but I will understand if you think it's too soon to meet your son, we can always do that another day, when you feel ready.'

'No, I'm ready, I'm just not sure if Daniel is, it's just; he has not seen me with any other man than his father and he has not seen him for the last few years, but that's how we like it, it's just me and him you see, me and him against the world, but I really had a nice weekend and I enjoyed every moment I spent with you.'

'Annette,' James reached over and took Annette's hand from her lap where she had been twisting her fingers nervously around each other. 'I knew you had a son, remember when we met in the supermarket and you were buying his birthday cake.' Annette nodded as she remembered. 'It never put me off you then and it really is not going to put me off you now, as for us meeting it's entirely down to you. I am happy to meet him and your parents today, or we can do it another day, like I said either way I am happy and will take no offence if that's what you're worried about.'

'Ok, today it is then.'

They both looked at each other 'lets do this thing' they said together and both fell into fits of laughter as they settled back and enjoyed the rest of the journey to Annette's parents house. As they pulled up outside Annette's parents' house, Annette swore she saw the curtains in the front room twitch. 'Oh they are here, quick is the house tidy enough? Would you believe it Frank look at the car he's driving.'

'Yes the house is tidy enough love, stop flapping, and stop looking out of that window before they notice they are being watched.' He had a quick glance out of the window himself as they opened the car's doors and got out. Hummm Aston Martin, Frank thought to himself not a bad little car I suppose.

Annette reached out and pressed the doorbell, James standing beside her, fiddling with his jacket zip, 'will you stop fussing' Annette told him, 'they don't bite you know' she said teasingly.

'Ok, ok, I just don't normally do the meet the parents thing and you're the first woman I have dated that's had a child, I just want to make a good impression that all.'

'Well you won't make a good anything if you keep fiddling like that.' Annette's mother opened the door to them, 'come in' she said.

'Mum, this is James.' Annette introduced James as they stepped in the front door and stood in the hall.

'Pleased to meet you James,' said Annette's mother as she closed the front door and turned around and held out her hand to shake James's hand,

'Likewise, Mrs. Johnson.'

'Call me Josephine or Josie, like everyone else does Mrs. Johnson makes me seem so old' as they both shook hands.

'Hello love,' Annette's mother said as she hugged her daughter.

'Hello mum.'

'Come in, come in,' she said to them both 'I will put the kettle on, your father and Daniel are in the front room, go on in.'

Daniel and Annette's father were both sitting on the sofa staring at a paused games console screen.

'Mum' said Daniel as he got up and hugged her; 'Daniel, dad, I would like you both to meet James.'

'Hi James' they both said,

'Frank' said Annette's dad as he shook hands with James.

'I am Daniel, do you play computer games?' Nanny said it was rude to be playing them when you got here so she made us put it on pause'.

'Urm,' replied James as he looked at Annette, she smiled and nodded her head. 'Actually I do and is that not the latest shoot em up your playing.'

'Yup, it sure is, mum got it for me as she felt guilty about leaving me all weekend.'

'Daniel,' gasped Annette 'That's not true.'

'Yes it is mum; you buy me a new game every time you go out with your new man here.'

Annette blushed, 'Can you take my mum out again next weekend?' Daniel asked James.

'Well that's up to your mum' James replied to him and they both turned and looked at Annette.

'I'm going to help nanny with the tea' Annette hurriedly said as she caught her dad's eye, he gave her a sly wink.

'Sit down James,' Annette's dad told him 'do you play?' as he offered James one of the console controllers.

'Yes actually I do play but have not had a chance to play this game yet.'

'I am going to beat you also, just like I have beaten granddad all weekend.'

'We will see about that' laughed James as he sat down on the sofa with control in hand.

In the end James and Annette had not only stayed for a cup of tea, they had also ordered a couple of take away pizzas for dinner, which Frank had insisted on paying for after turning down James offer of at least paying for his own. It was evening time by the time Annette and everyone else had said goodbye to James, Annette sighed as she shut the front door after waving goodbye, just after Daniel had caught them kissing and had serenaded them with a loud, 'Mummy and James sitting in a tree K.I.S.S.I.N.G.'

'Daniel!'

Annette and her mother had both said at once. Daniel and James had both laughed as Daniel went back into the front room to finish 'whooping granddad's backside' as he had put it.

Chapter Twenty Six

Annette and Daniel were now back at home, sitting together in the front room, snuggled up on the sofa watching a film and eating microwave popcorn Annette had found in the back of the kitchen cupboard. Daniel had been asking loads of questions about Annette's weekend and Annette had been filling him in on everything.

It was October half term and Annette had booked the week off work to spend with Daniel, so she did not mind how late it got as she knew that on Monday morning neither of them had to go anywhere, actually they did not have to go anywhere until Wednesday when she had promised to take Daniel swimming; so Monday and Tuesday could be pyjama and movie days. They had been talking about James and Daniel had asked if James was her boyfriend, she told him yes he was a boy and he was a friend so yes he was her boyfriend Daniel looked at her and rolled his eyes.

'That's not what I meant mum, I meant is he your boyfriend, boyfriend!'

Annette looked at her son and realised he was growing up fast, 'in answer to your boyfriend, boyfriend question, then yes, I suppose he is my boyfriend, boyfriend.'

'Ooooo' Daniel began before jumping up from the sofa and doing a dance around the front room singing again: 'Mummy and James sitting in a tree K.I.S.S.I.N.G!' Annette laughed as she watched her son doing the silly dance.

Daniel stopped dancing and looked at Annette with a serious look in his eyes 'Does that mean he will be my new dad?' He said in a quiet voice.

'Well, sit down again will you' Annette said in a soft voice. Daniel did what he was told and sat back down next to his mum, 'I like him very much and I think he likes me, but him becoming your new dad as you put it will be a long way off, if it happens at all.'

'Shame' replied Daniel.

'Shame?' repeated Annette slightly confused,

'Yes, it's a shame I would not mind him for a dad, he is really cool and he let me beat him at the computer game.'

'Well if anything like that happens I promise you will be the first to know.'

'Now time for bed Mr, it's very late and you may not be tired but I am shattered, at least we can both have a lie in the morning.

'Ok mum night,' Daniel got up from the sofa gave Annette a hug and a kiss goodnight and went upstairs to bed leaving Annette staring at the credits rolling up the TV screen from the end of the film.

Chapter Twenty Seven

On Monday morning Annette awoke to the sound of gunfire coming from Daniel's bedroom; she checked her clock for the time, half past ten, thank goodness neither of them had to be anywhere or they both would have been very late. 'Breakfast time Daniel,' Annette called out as she wrapped her dressing gown around herself, not as soft as the one in the hotel room she thought and decided that this afternoon she would go shopping with Daniel for some new clothes and treat herself to a new dressing gown. As Annette was making her breakfast she noticed her mobile flashing on the side, where she had put it down next to her bags after coming home last night. She picked it up and checked her messages she had six! Two were from James, three were from Maddie. She read James's texts first, one was sent last night - *Thank you for a great weekend, I really enjoyed myself and your family are great, really enjoyed meeting them and I especially loved the k.i.s.s.i.n.g song by Daniel. You have a great kid there and I was honoured to meet him, I know how much courage that must have taken.* The second text was sent this morning, *do you fancy meeting up sometime today, I can take a couple hours off work is Daniel allowed McDonald's ? My treat!*

The three texts from Maddie read - *tell me everything now or else! I am dying to hear the full story - What happened with bitch face?* And, *talk to me woman going spare waiting to hear all the juicy bits.*

Annette laughed and as she told Daniel to turn off the console as breakfast was ready she text Maddie back. *Nothing to tell weekend was great, James was great, and thanks to you I put bitch face in her place, oh and by the way James met my parents and Daniel last night!* And with that Annette pressed send.

Needless to say Maddie called Annette within thirty seconds of receiving her text and demanded the full story there and then. Annette took the call in her bedroom as she did not want Daniel overhearing how James made her feel. She told Maddie everything; she could hear from her tone that Maddie was grinning from ear to ear. Annette checked that Daniel was downstairs watching TV, before she took a deep breath and told Maddie about the solicitor's letter she had received this morning, she had filed for divorce and Simon had received the papers on Saturday. Saturday the day of the wedding, one of the happiest days Annette had had in a long, long time. 'Oh Annette' Maddie had said at last when Annette had told her, 'How do you your feel about it?'

'I think I am relieved, I don't know, i'm not too sure what I am feeling to be honest.'

As Annette recalled Simon's vicious words 'if you ever try to leave me, I will kill you!' she shuddered.

'Annette? are you still there, you ok?'

'Yes I am still here;' there was a moment of silence when neither Annette nor Maddie knew quite what to say, then Maddie broke the silence 'does James know?'

'No; James knows nothing about Simon, I want to tell him, to be truthful with him, but I can't find the right time or the right words to say "oh by the way I am married," it did not quite fit in with any conversations we have had.'

'Tell him when you're ready' was Maddie's advice.

'I will, and talking of James,' said Annette, 'we are supposed to be meeting him in McDonald's in about half hour and I am still not dressed!'

'We' enquired Maddie.

'Me and Daniel, James is going to treat us to lunch.'

'Ok, you best get ready then and Annette, try not to worry I am sure everything will work out for the best, you know I am here for you anytime.'

'I know, thank you Maddie.'

'You're welcome, full update required later though.'

Annette laughed 'of course I will call you when I'm home.'

Annette finished the phone call and called down to Daniel, 'Are you ready yet? We are going to be late.'

Annette and Daniel had made it on time, just about as they had decided to walk. James was already waiting outside for them both after giving Annette a quick peck to the cheek they all went inside for lunch.

After they had finished James turned to Daniel and said 'I have a surprise for you' Annette and Daniel both looked at James as he reached into a small plastic bag he had sitting next to him.

'Surprise!' announced James as he pulled out what looked like a computer game and handed it over to Daniel.

'Oh wow mum look' Daniel said to his mother as he held the game in his hand 'it's the new car racing game it only came out this morning - can we all go back to ours and play it now?'

'Well Daniel, I am not sure, James is probably busy and needs to get back to work.'

'Actually, I took the afternoon off work and if it's ok with you I thought we could go back to mine, I have everything set up and waiting, just need the game and someone to play with now.'

Daniel and James both turned to look at Annette and they had the puppy look in their eyes as Daniel said *'pleeeeeeeeeease,'* Annette looked from one to the other before finally sighing 'well I suppose that's ok. But not for long.'

'Yesssssss' both James and Daniel said at once.

Chapter Twenty Eight

They left and made their way to James's apartment. James and Daniel had raced to the corner of the road, which was also where the High Street ended; James's apartment block was on the other side of the road, James had let Daniel win and by the time Annette had joined them both, Daniel was teasing James on being too old to beat a eleven year old. As they crossed the road Annette looked up at the building, it was the same building that Annette had seen every day as she walked into work; the picture of the building was on the office wall along with lots of other pictures of buildings. As they walked through the main doors Annette took in the lobby area, there was a large oval shaped desk in the middle of the back wall and behind it stood a security guard, and next to him either side were two lifts, the whole lobby area was carpeted in thick pile carpet it was warm and inviting. James looked at Annette unsure of what the expression on her face meant. 'I am guessing Carrington's pays you a lot more then they pay me' said Annette, and a thin smile played on her lips. 'About that' James began determined to tell Annette how the company was actually owned by his parents but run by himself.

'Daniel, stop!' Annette exclaimed and moved towards the lift where Daniel was getting in, 'wait for us, you don't know where you are going and judging by the size of the building I really don't want you getting lost.'

'Don't be silly mum, I am not that stupid, I was just going to hold the lift for you both and besides James is carrying the computer game!'

'Can I press the button?' Daniel asked as they both joined him in the lift, 'which floor?'

Annette looked at the array of buttons on the display in front of her; they were numbered 1-15.

'Press the top one,' James instructed Daniel.

'Number 15?' enquired Daniel.

'No, the top one.'

'But that's blank' said Daniel confused.

'Yup, press the blank one' Daniel did what he was told and pressed the blank one and the lift started to move upwards. They all stood in silence as they watched the display counting up the floors and Annette was wondering what would happen once they had reached 15; Annette did not have to wait long to find out that after 15 a red letter P appeared on the display as the lift came to a stop.

As the doors opened they all got out and walked from the lift on to the landing. Annette looked up and down she realised there was only one door on the whole level.

'Come on in' said James as he opened the only door on that level. 'Welcome to my humble abode.' There was nothing humble about it at all thought Annette, as they all stepped inside, the carpets were cream as were the walls. As Annette took her shoes off inside the front door she silently thanked God she was wearing clean socks with no holes in, as Daniel took his shoes off she was equally reassured that Daniel too was wearing clean socks with no holes in; as she put her now socked feet on the carpet it was thick and felt so soft under Annette's feet, James and Daniel had already gone through the archway on her right and Annette noticed that there was two other doors on her left and one straight in front of her. Annette followed them through the archway and walked into the large front room where Daniel was already sitting in front of a huge TV screen, James was in the kitchen at the far end of the front room, raised up slightly from the front room itself by a small step.

'Tea, coffee or something else?' James asked Annette as she sat down on the plush sofa Daniel was already on. 'No thank you, I am fine.'

'Daniel?' James asked 'do you want anything?'

'Have you any coke?' Daniel answered back '

'I have if that's ok with your mum' and James looked at Annette 'ok but just the one' she answered. Daniel had already had one coke with his lunch and Annette did not wish Daniel to start getting hyped up on the caffeine.

'Can or glass?' enquired James

'Can!' 'Glass!'

Answered Daniel and Annette respectively 'Sorry, glass it is then mate, I don't want to be in your mum's bad books now do I? As Annette watched James grab a can of coke out of the fridge she could not help but feel slightly jealous; the fridge was one of the huge American style fridges that Annette could only dream about affording, let alone fit in her kitchen, she would have to remove far too many cupboards and remove too much work surface to fit one of them in. James poured Daniel's can of coke into a glass and did the same with his and made his way to join them on the sofa. James gave Daniel the honours of loading up the new game into the console.

In the end Annette and Daniel stayed all afternoon and Annette was saying how they should really be going as it was getting late and she needed to go home and cook her and Daniel's dinner, 'what are you having?' enquired James.

'I am not too sure actually' Annette thought about the contents of her small fridge freezer and cupboards, she really needed to do a shop!

'Well I was having a take away and you are welcome to join me.'

'Can we mum, can we please?'

'I don't know Daniel, we have been here all afternoon and I am sure James must have better things to be doing than sitting here with us.'

'There is nothing more I would rather be doing than sitting here with you both and I need to beat Daniel just one more time to make up for my appalling lap time last time round.'

'Yer, you can try Mr,' laughed Daniel.

'Please mum please.' Daniel begged his mum.

'Ok, but I need to be home by 8 pm as I am not missing the comedy on TV tonight.'

'*Yessssss*' said Daniel and James together.

In the end 8pm came and went; they had ordered an Indian meal and watched the comedy together, somewhere along the line Annette had found that she and James were now holding hands as Daniel sat on the floor, stroking a fluffy grey cat that had come wandering in. James had explained it was one of his mother's cats and when his parents had moved abroad she had asked James to look after it for her, which James had agreed to.

It was 10pm by the time Annette and Daniel had got a cab home. As Annette got into bed that night she was feeling on top of the world.

Chapter Twenty Nine

Annette awoke early Tuesday morning before the alarm went off, she woke up and smiled as she remembered yesterday, she looked at the clock 8am, not too bad. Annette got out of bed and got wrapped in her dressing gown and went downstairs, she paused outside Daniel's bedroom door on her way to the bathroom and heard nothing, not even one beep from any form of computerised equipment.

Annette made her way into the kitchen, humming softly to herself, as she looked in the cupboards and fridge to decide on breakfast; she realised she was not all that hungry so she decided to just have a nice cup of tea and a piece of toast, at half eight she had finished her breakfast and still no noise to be heard from Daniel's room so she decided to cook Daniel a fry up, she had eggs, mushrooms and tomatoes and not forgetting the bacon and beans she had also found. She turned on the small radio that lived in the kitchen and while cooking Daniel's breakfast she also danced and sang, quietly of course. Daniel finally came downstairs at 9am which was perfect timing as she had even managed to unearth a couple of sausages at the back of the freezer to add to the mountain of breakfast she was already cooking for him. Daniel tucked into his breakfast and between mouthfuls Annette and Daniel figured out their plan for the day, Daniel wanted to go swimming but Annette wanted to re-paint the hallway downstairs, the hallway was a pale yellow but Annette wanted a nice vibrant yellow to match the colour of the kitchen. Annette promised Daniel they could go swimming tomorrow providing of course Daniel helped her paint, and, as she pointed out to him, how could he say no after the lovely breakfast she had slaved over for him all morning. Daniel finally agreed to the painting today and swimming tomorrow 'on one condition' Daniel said 'Hummm' replied Annette looking at Daniel 'can James come too?'

'Daniel, just because you have a week off school and I managed to book the week off work does not mean everyone can just take days off whenever they want you know,'

'I know that mum, but he does not need to take the whole day off, just the afternoon or even a couple of hours will do mum, you will ask him wont you?'

'Ok I will at least ask him, if I hear from him that is, but don't get your hopes up just in case he can't make it.'

'Okay mum I won't.'

'Now we need to go and get dressed, in old clothes, and then let's crack on with the painting.'

Annette did not really want James to come swimming with them, she did not like the idea of James seeing her semi naked even though Annette was planning on wearing her black all in one swimming costume it did not matter, he would still see the tops of her legs, her wobbly thighs and she did not feel ready for James to see that much of her, but she told Daniel she would ask, so she will do. Annette had already heard from James this morning, when she had come downstairs she grabbed her phone out of her handbag which she had left in the kitchen and had a text from him already, much to Annette's embarrassment the text had simply read *morning sexy x*. Annette had not wanted to seem too eager so she had waited till now to text him back, *morning to you too*. Annette had started to text back, before she had a chance to finish she almost dropped the phone in shock as it rang in her hand, 'Hello' Annette said.

'Hello. May I speak to a Ms. Johnson' came back a strange voice at the other end of the phone.

'Speaking' said Annette frowning at the phone.

'This is Mr. West calling from the solicitor's office, how are you today?'

'I am fine' said Annette she was now a bit stumped as to why he was calling, perhaps he was just checking I received the letter she reasoned to herself. 'I am afraid I have some bad news for you Ms. Johnson, are you ok to continue the conversation or would you prefer if I called back later?'

'No, no, now's fine' as she sat down on the kitchen chair.

'I had a rather short conversation with your husband and the gist of the conversation is; he won't sign the papers.'

'What do you mean he won't sign the papers?'

'I am sorry Ms Johnson that's just what he said, well I am leaving out the swearwords he used of course.'

'Was he really angry?' Annette asked.

'To be honest, yes he was rather angry, I did try to talk to him but he slammed the phone down on me. Sorry Ms Johnson.'

'No, no that's ok, well I mean it's not ok that he won't sign them, I just mean it's not your fault.'

Annette sighed and slumped down on her chair, any excitement she had felt this morning drained away, she felt like a huge black cloud had descended above her head and was about to pour down with rain all over her.

'Sorry again Ms. Johnson, but we can try again in a couple of months, he may have changed his mind by then, after years years we can proceed without him anyway, are you ok Ms. Johnson, Ms. Johnson?'

'Yes, I am still here, he, he won't be able to find us will he?' asked Annette.

'No he won't be able to find you, well not through us anyway, we don't give out personal information not to anyone and even more so in your case Ms. Johnson, we take domestic violence cases very seriously, so even if he showed up at our offices and held a gun to my head, I would still not be able to give over any of your details.'

'Thank you Mr. West that has made me feel a bit better.' It had not really made her feel any better but it seemed polite thing to say at the time.

'I will be in touch if I hear anything else Ms Johnson.'

'Ok, thank you Mr. West, for letting me know.'

As Annette put the phone down she rested her head on the table and cried.

'Ready mum?' Said Daniel, as he bounced down the stairs a couple of minutes later 'who was that on the phone? Was it James, is he coming?'

Annette sniffed and turned her back to Daniel as she quickly used the back of her hands to wipe away the tears.

'No it was not James darling, it was someone else,'

'You ok mum' asked Daniel 'you look like you've been crying,'

'I am ok Daniel, why don't you go and watch a bit of TV while I tidy the kitchen,'

'Are you sure your ok mum?'

'Yes darling, now go put the TV on before I make you do the washing up' said Annette who managed a smile just to show Daniel she was ok and with Annette's last comment, Daniel dashed off into the front room and turned on the TV.

Annette had done the washing up and had made herself another cup of tea she was upstairs in her bedroom on the phone to Maddie telling her everything the solicitor had just said.

Chapter Thirty

In the end Annette and Daniel had not done any of the painting, Daniel had decided to go and see a couple of his friends and had made her promise she was going to ask James about swimming tomorrow. "James" Annette did not want to think about him right now, the glow she had felt this morning had long gone as she was starting to wonder if seeing James was the right thing to do at all, but she had promised Daniel so she did it the coward's way and text him. She got a reply almost immediately, *have a meeting in the afternoon but could meet you for a bite to eat after if that's ok.* Annette text back - *ok*.

Chapter Thirty One

Annette had been awake most of the night as Tuesday turned into Wednesday. Daniel had got back from his friend's house after tea; they just sat on the sofa and watched TV together before going to bed. Daniel was excited to hear that, although James could not come swimming with them, he was going to meet them after. Annette wondered as she looked at the grin on Daniel's face if she was going to be doing the right or wrong thing, Annette did not really know what to think about anything. She had laid in bed for hours just listening to the sounds of the clock ticking and the sound of the occasional car going past; being with James had made her so happy but it had also side tracked her from what was more important and right now that was Daniel, even though Daniel was happy to have James around.

Annette had to sort this business with Simon out, she wanted that man out of their lives once and for all and then Annette decided she could really move on. It was around 3am when Annette finally drifted off to sleep only to have nightmares where one minute she would be kissing James and then James would suddenly turn into Simon laughing at her and she felt him pushing her down a flight of stairs. As

Annette woke she was hot with sweat, she checked the time 6.30am and she decided that she'd had enough of trying to sleep and went and had a nice refreshing shower and changed her bed sheets, so by the time Daniel was up at 9am she had already laid the breakfast table and was drinking her second cup of coffee.

Daniel was asking what time they were going swimming and what time they were meeting James. Annette did not really want to think about James, she wanted; needed to get her head and feelings straight, she was wondering if she was just being stupid when it came to James, he was a good looking single bloke and here she was a single mother with a eleven year old son and a past he knew nothing about. What did she really know about James, not a lot she concluded, she knew he worked for Carrington's or at least she knew he looked at properties and passed them on to her bosses at Carrington's and she knew he lived in one of the buildings Carrington's owned but then so did lots of other people, that's how Carrington's made their money she guessed. They bought run down properties and sold them on once they had been transformed into luxury apartments. It was just after 1.30pm by the time she and Daniel had made it out of the house. Annette had tried to call Maddie a couple of times, but had no reply, they had reached the swimming baths by 2pm and were meeting James at 4pm in the restaurant just across the road from the swimming baths. It was fun swim that afternoon at the swimming pool, which meant they had all the floats, giant ones and small ones, rubber rings, and blown up crocodiles and sharks to play with in the water. Annette watched with amusement as Daniel and a couple of other guys Daniel knew from school where piling the large swimming mats on top of each other and were all trying to climb on board without the mats tipping over and dunking them all back in the pool. Annette had swum a few lengths up and down and deciding that Daniel did not actually need her watching over him, she signalled to Daniel he had half an hour left and she was getting out. As Annette stood under the surprisingly hot swimming pool showers for a change, her tummy was beginning to do tummy flips in anticipation of seeing James in less than an hour, providing Daniel remembered to get out of the pool and be ready on time.

Annette was sitting in the small café area at the swimming pool, reading today's newspaper that someone had kindly left behind, when Daniel appeared, dressed and he had even managed to comb his still wet hair. Annette looked at her watch ten minutes to go, they had better walk over the road now; she was leaving the car in the car park as it seemed silly to move it just from one side of the road to the other and she still had a bit of time left until the car parking ticket she had bought ran out. James was already inside, seated at a table, when they arrived He got up when he saw them come in, 'Hello Daniel' James said as they both sat down opposite him at the table. 'Hello to you too' he leaned over the table to give Annette a peck on the cheek, which sent a shiver of lust down her spine as she felt his soft lips on her cheek, 'Yum you smell appley' said James once he had sat back down, 'Thank you' was all Annette could say back as the waiter arrived to take their order. James and Daniel ordered burger and chips and Annette ordered a sandwich for herself as she found she was not very hungry; as they ate Annette found herself not knowing what to say and every question James passed in her direction she found one word answers for. In the end James and Daniel were discussing computer games. Do boys ever grow up Annette thought to herself?

Annette managed to leave just after they had all finished, her mind today, not comprehending the small talk. James had insisted on paying and Annette really did not have the energy to argue with him. As they all walked outside James caught Annette by the arm and pulled her to him, 'Are you ok?' James had a concerned look on his face as he asked her in such a soft tone. Annette thought she might melt into the ground at any moment. 'I am not feeling too good' lied

Annette 'And my car parking ticket is due to run out I really don't wish to get clamped.'

'Shall I call you later? or you can call me?, I will be in all evening' he kissed her softly and gently on the lips 'Careful you don't want to catch anything off me' said Annette as it took all her will to pull away from him.

'Yuck!' said Daniel.

Chapter Thirty Two

They managed to be home just after 5pm, Daniel had been sulking slightly in the car on the way home, he thought that they had left too early and was going on about how much he liked James and when could they see him again, just as they pulled up outside Annette snapped at Daniel 'He's not your dad you know so stop bloody going on about him!' She turned and saw Daniel's eyes filling with tears and instantly felt guilty 'Oh Daniel I am so sorry, Daniel please, I never meant too…..'

'Yes you did' yelled Daniel as he got out of the thankfully now motionless car.

'Oh Daniel, please listen to me, please' Annette tried saying as she unlocked the front door, Daniel raced past her and up the stairs where he slammed his bedroom door shut. Annette shut the front door and ran upstairs after him. 'Daniel' she said softly as she tapped on his closed bedroom door.

'Go away' she heard a muffled reply from his room.

'Daniel please let me talk to you, let me explain.'

'I said, GO AWAY!' with tears filling in her eyes Annette walked away from Daniel's bedroom door and went downstairs.

Annette must have dozed off on the sofa as she was aware someone else was in the room with her, she looked up with a fright to see Daniel standing over her, his eyes were red from crying and her heart went out to him. 'I am so sorry' she said reaching up to hug Daniel, 'You're right though mum he's not my dad.'

'I am sorry, I never meant it to come out like that, I have just had a lot on my mind over the last couple of days and I should never have shouted at you like that, I promise I will never do it again,' as Daniel sat down next to his mum and returned the hug.

'I don't feel very well' he whispered, Annette used the back of her hand and felt his head.

'You do feel a bit warm, it's probably all that water you drank out of the swimming pool' and they both laughed 'come on lets go to bed.'

Annette was lying on her bed, Daniel was now fast asleep in his own bed, as she checked on him, she knew what she had to do, it was 10pm and she had been lying on her bed thinking for the last two hours but she needed to do it quick before she changed her mind. She picked up her phone and called Maddie.

'Can you come over and watch Daniel for me' Annette blurted out as soon as Maddie answered the phone.

'When?'

'Now!.'

'Now?' repeated Maddie.

'Look Madz there is something I need to do and I need to do it now before I change my mind.'

'Okay, say no more, give me twenty minutes and I'll be right with you.'

'Thanks Maddie.'

True to her word Maddie was there in twenty minutes, which gave Annette enough time to grab the nearest clothes to throw on, which were a pair of blue jeans and an old cream sweater.

'Is everything ok' Maddie asked when she arrived at the door.

'It will be, I hope.'

'You go do what you have to do, where is Daniel?'

'He is asleep in his bed, he did say he was not feeling too good but I gave him a couple of painkillers and he went to sleep around 8pm, so he should be fine, I will have my mobile with me.' said Annette as she held up her mobile in case Maddie did not believe her. 'I should not be too long, about an hour.'

'We will be fine.'

Annette got into her car and started the engine, she really hoped she was going to do the right thing, she was going to tell James that they were no longer an item, she was just going to explain that she had other things on her mind and although she really liked him a lot, it was just bad timing on her part right now As she drove closer and closer to his apartment she really hoped he was actually in, her hands were shaking when she locked the car up outside the apartment block. Normally during the day you could not park around here but there was normally three or four spare car parking bays at this time of night. James had told her he parks in the underground car park under the block but Annette did not want to risk that; she took a deep breath and walked in the building, the security guard glanced up at her as she walked in, Annette was relieved to see that it was the same security guard that had been on the other day when they had first seen James's apartment. He smiled as Annette walked to the lift and pressed the button. Annette smiled back and got into the lift, her heart was beating wildly and the palms of her hands were getting sweaty as she reached up and pushed the blank button on the display, she tried to focus her breathing and was running through what she was going to say, it's not you, it's me, how could she use that line, no she was going to stick to what she had agreed with herself earlier. Annette felt sick as the lift reached the top and the red P came up on the display to signal she had reached the top floor.

Chapter Thirty Three

Annette used every ounce of courage she had to knock at the door, her mind was furiously running through what she was going to say as James opened the door she saw the look of surprise register on his face as he took in her standing at his doorway late at night. 'James I' she began she never got a chance to say another word as James pulled her into him and began to kiss her firmly on the lips and as she felt herself melt into his body all the words she had planned to say melted away. James, still kissing her, walked backwards into his bedroom and began to move his hands up her jumper and with one swift movement her bra was undone and he slipped her jumper off over her head, dropped her bra and jumper on the floor. Annette had no doubt in her mind she wanted to be ravaged by James and she wanted him badly, like she had wanted no one else before. They fell on the bed as James tugged off her jeans, she gasped as James moved her knickers aside and used his tongue to make her wet, her body felt like it was no longer part of her, she grabbed hold of his hair and let out a soft moan, as he worked his way up her body covering her with gentle kisses he flicked his tongue over her already hard, erect nipples, he kissed her hard on the lips as she wrapped her legs around his back and pulled him close to her, she felt his solid hard cock rub against her, when he entered her she pushed herself into him as far as she could go, his body was everything and more than Annette had imagined. He was strong, but gentle and as she felt the waves of an orgasm coming on she dug her nails into his back as James pushed faster and harder into her, she screamed in ecstasy as the waves of her orgasm ran through her body. They were both wet with sweat and still breathless when Annette heard a tune sounding out in the quiet of his apartment. 'Shit!, that's my phone' exclaimed Annette as she jumped out of bed and scrabbled on the floor to find her jeans where her phone was still ringing, 'Hello' Annette quickly said into the phone. 'Oh God, I am so sorry,' came Maddie's voice at the other end 'It's Daniel' she added. 'Oh my God what's wrong?' Annette started pulling on her clothes while still listening to the phone. 'He keeps being sick and is asking for you, sorry.' 'Don't be sorry I am on my way.' Annette grabbed her clothes and turned to James while pulling on her jeans, 'It's Daniel he's ill, I have got to go.'

'That's ok I understand, hope Daniel's ok.'

No he's not thought Annette as she picked up her shoes and left the apartment she got back in the lift that was thankfully still on James's floor. She put her shoes on in the lift and ran from the lift outside to her car; as she got in her car she realised they had not used any form of protection, disgusted with herself for behaving like she was a teenage hussy, for not only using no protection, but for leaping on him the way she did. She shuddered, as she remembered telling him to fuck her hard. Oh my God did I really say that, what must he think of me as she drove off back home as fast as she could.

Chapter Thirty Four

Daniel and Annette had both finally got to sleep at 4am Thursday morning, Maddie had left around 1am after Annette insisting she was fine and could manage and as Maddie had to work the next morning Annette sent her home with assurances that if she needed her, she would call and Maddie could come straight back. Daniel had been throwing up for over three hours, Annette just sat with him on the bathroom floor with a cold flannel she was wiping over his head, as he was sick over and over again until his poor body had nothing left. They climbed into Annette's bed and they fell into an exhausted sleep. Annette awoke the next morning when Daniel started being sick again. Once again Annette sat on the bathroom floor with him rubbing his back as he retched into the toilet just bringing up the small amount of water he had drunk. Annette hated herself even more, her son needed her and where was she, in someone else's bed lying on her back and on top at one point she reminded herself. She rinsed out the flannel and wiped it over Daniel's hot, sweaty brow, as she reminded herself she must get the morning after pill; she tucked Daniel up in his own bed changed the sheets on hers, Daniel's sweat had soaked the bedding, she checked on Daniel who was sleeping again and walked back into her room, she laid down on her freshly changed bed sheets and fell asleep.

When Annette woke again she noticed it was dark outside. Annette sat up and upon checking the clock she noticed it was 7pm, she walked into Daniel's room he was still sleeping; as she turned to walk out of his room, she heard a small voice 'Mummy, water please,' was all Daniel could manage. Annette helped him to drink a few mouthfuls of water, sponged off his head and went downstairs to get a couple more painkillers for him, she walked past the front room and noticed the answer machine flashing, someone must have called when they were asleep this afternoon, I will deal with it tomorrow she decided, as she took the painkillers and a fresh bottle of water up for Daniel, she promised herself to get the morning after pill in the morning.

They both woke late Friday morning, Annette quietly went into check on Daniel; as she knelt down next to his bed, she could smell sick and sweat, she felt his head and he was still burning, Daniel half opened his eyes, 'Water' he croaked, 'Please mummy.' Annette sat him up and passed him the water, 'Would you like me to run you a nice hot bath?' Daniel nodded 'Please.' While Daniel was in the bath Annette changed his bed sheets; the morning after pill will have to wait until tomorrow. She did not want to leave

Daniel and she did not want the embarrassment of asking anyone else to buy it for her, she did not even want Maddie to know, how she had behaved like such a slut.

She tucked Daniel back into bed after he had a quick bath, he was shivering with cold by the time he got out the bath. Annette sat by the bed stroking his head and singing to him just like she used to when he was a baby. It was midday by the time Annette went downstairs and as she walked past the front room door she remembered the answer phone; she walked in and pressed play. James's sexy deep voice filled the room, 'Hi it's me, James, hope Daniel is ok, you have my number if you need me.' Annette hit the delete button and walked out of the front room. How could she have been so stupid, things were much easier when it was just her and Daniel and that's how it was going to stay, she decided, as she walked into the kitchen and turned the kettle on. Daniel woke up a couple of hours later, Annette had managed to call Maddie to let her know Daniel was on the mend and she also managed to call her mother who passed on her love and get well soon messages to Daniel. Daniel had managed half a piece of toast and a drink of cold lemonade, flat lemonade, as the doctor who had come and done a home visit advised her. Gastroenteritis he diagnosed, while informing her that it normally takes 1-10 days for it to clear up and warned Annette that as gastroenteritis is highly contagious she is more than likely to get it herself. Sure enough that evening Annette was bent over the bathroom toilet and that's where she stayed for most of the evening before dragging herself to bed at some point during the night.

Chapter Thirty Five

By Monday morning, they were both feeling better, to be on the safe side Annette had called in sick both for herself and for Daniel as it was his first day back at school after half term and it was supposed to be her first day back at work. Luckily Tom did not mind and completely understood when Annette explained she had caught it from her son, and yes she was ok but was giving it one more day to be on the safe side rather than spreading it around the Carrington offices. The school secretary simply said 'There's a lot of that going around at the moment look forward to having him back tomorrow'.

Annette could not believe how quick the month of November had flown by, Daniel and herself had resumed normal routine from the second of November. It had been a tough month as Annette tried to avoid James, when James was around she tried to ignore him, by the time she did have to speak to him it was middle of November and he had come in for a meeting with Tom but was half an hour early. He tried to talk to Annette as she worked on the desk and she tried to avoid his eyes; when their eyes did meet James's were full of hurt, she could see the pain in them and she knew she was to blame for it, which did not help her at all. Daniel had asked after James a couple of times and she had been honest with him and told him that they were not boyfriend and girlfriend any longer. Daniel accepted that explanation, with a simple shrug of his shoulders and a one word comment 'Shame!'

It was now the first Saturday in December and Annette was surrounded by Christmas cards and her Christmas card list, Daniel was out with some friends, they had gone to play football in the park after lunch. Annette had not been feeling to good over the last couple of days she had been very tired and feeling sick, so this quiet time to herself was just what she needed. As she sat back and started to write her Christmas cards, the phone rang, Annette sighed as she went to answer it: 'hello, hello, anyone there? Hello?' Annette put the phone down and got back to writing her Christmas cards. By the time Daniel had got home at tea time Annette had finished writing all the cards and was feeling much better; stress; she had put the tiredness down to, along with the sickness feeling.

The following weekend Maddie had come over for a girl's night in and as Annette was describing how she had been feeling Maddie looked at her and raised her eyebrows,

Annette looked at Maddie 'what? why you looking at me like that for?'

'Tiredness, sickness, sore boobs, dizzy spells.'

'The dizzy spells have passed; I never told you I had sore boobs, did I?'

'The sore boobs was just a guess.'

'What, wait you don't think I am, do you?'

'Well you have ticked off most of the symptoms.'

'Don't be so silly, I can't be?'

Annette tipped out the contents of her handbag on the front room floor in front of where they were both sitting and grabbed her diary and started to flick back a few pages, 'Ah ah, see I can't be' said Annette flashing her diary in front of Maddie and pointing at a small dot on the day marked 9th November 'What about for this month?' asked Maddie.

'No I have not had a period yet but I was only due on at the start of this week, you know I have been stressed which is why I might be a few days late and as I have sore boobs that must be a sign I am due on.'

'If you say so' sung Maddie.

'Now shut up, and tell me all about Dale.' Annette said changing the subject swiftly.

As Maddie told Annette all about Dale who was the latest love of Maddie's life, Annette thought back through the dates in her diary and with a dreadful feeling in the pit of her stomach she remembered the period she'd had back in November just being a light one, not like the kind of bleeding she normally has, this was light and over in a couple of days, when normally hers are 6-7 days long. Annette concentrated on what Maddie was saying and pushed all thoughts of pregnancy out of her head, when Annette woke the next morning she decided to get a pregnancy test, and as it was a Sunday her chemist was not open so it would have to wait. On Wednesday she managed to go to the supermarket and picked up a pack of two tests, she hid them in the drawer under her bed once she got home. She was going to do one that evening, but by the time she had cooked dinner and put the shopping away it was too late and anyway it said on the pack to use the first morning urine sample. As it happened Annette forgot the next morning and with a trembling hand, once Daniel had gone to bed she pee'd on the stick, put the lid back on, closed her eyes and counted to sixty.

Chapter Thirty Six

Oh my God, 2 lines, Shit two lines, No, Hold on, Don't panic, Two lines is good, thought Annette as she reached for the slip of paper with the instructions written on, Shit! No! Two lines are not good, not good at all, Shit! As the bit of paper fluttered to the floor, Annette had not needed to check it as the memories of standing in the bathroom with Simon's arms wrapped around her as they both saw the 2 lines appear in the window of the test to confirm her pregnancy with Daniel. As memories came flooding back, Annette bent over the toilet and was violently sick.

Chapter Thirty Seven

Annette awoke and glanced over at the clock, 'damn,' 'Daniel, I forgot to set my alarm, we are running late Daniel! Daniel!'

'I'm up, I'm up' came a response finally from Daniel's bedroom.

'Were you ok last night mum, I heard you throwing up?' Daniel asked her as they were both in the kitchen grabbing a packet of crisps each to eat on the way to school and work.

'I am fine now, it must have been something dodgy I ate last night, don't forget your gym kit.'

'Where is my gym kit?' Daniel yelled having run from the kitchen to upstairs.

'By the front door, you just walked past it.'

'Are you ready now?' she asked him as they both stood by the front door.

'Yup, let's go mum.'

Annette made it into work five minutes late and found Claire sitting at her desk. 'Are you ok?' Asked Claire as Annette rushed in the doors 'Are you ok?' She asked again. 'I was holding the fort for you, I told anyone who asked that you had nipped to the loo, hope that was ok?'

'Oh thank you Claire' Annette replied dumping her bag behind the desk and hugged her.

'Now get your act together. Big boss is due in for meeting at 9.15 this morning.'

'No one told me!' Gasped Annette.

'Did you not read the email that got sent yesterday?'

'No, what email?' and as Annette checked through her emails there it was with the unread envelope picture sitting next to it.

What happened in the next two minutes confused Annette. James, Tom and another man Annette had never seen before walked in, Claire left Annette's side and shaking hands with all three men she led them to the lift. Annette looked at her computer screen Claire had opened up a blank page on the computer screen and had typed, he is so gorgeous, would not mind seeing what is under them clothes at all x x with a winking face. Now Annette was confused as far as she could see, the big boss must have been the man she had not met before but he was in his 50's at a guess, was balding and from what Annette could tell he had a beer belly not so well hidden under his ill fitted shirt. She emailed Claire and asked who she thought was gorgeous. *Our big boss man?* Finally the end of Friday came and as Annette checked her emails one last time still no reply from Claire, she guessed it must be a pretty big meeting going on as she had not seen any of the three men leaving, unless they had left when she was at lunch which could have been possible. She turned off the computer, grabbed her bag from under the desk and left the building.

Chapter Thirty Eight

James woke up Saturday morning feeling like rubbish he had, had a bit too much to drink last night and had the hangover to prove it, it had been over seven weeks since he last spoke to Annette properly and it was killing him. Every time he saw her he wanted to envelope her in a giant hug and never left her go, it was not only hugging he wanted to do to her, he wanted to pick her up and carry her away somewhere quiet with just them and Daniel and live happily ever after. He decided that tonight he would go around and knock on the door and ask to speak to her; she had avoided all his calls and had not returned any of his texts or phone calls. The only reply he got back was when a week after Daniel had been ill, he asked if Daniel was any better, to which she had just replied, *yes*, so James had left it at that, but tonight he was going around and was not going to leave until she had heard what he had to say. He had made his mind up, tonight was the night.

Annette and Daniel had decided that today was the day that All things Christmas where being put up in the house and they were going to make some mince pies, but first they had to go and buy a Christmas tree. Annette and Daniel had a great day it had taken them a couple of hours to find the right tree but they found it and now it was in the front room with the twinkling lights and tinsel wrapped around it, the Christmas lights were up on the front room window and Annette had even managed to hang some outside. It was their first Christmas together in the house and Annette was going to make sure it was a special one for them both as this time next year it would be the three of them she thought as she rubbed her hand over the bump that was just starting to form. She had woken up this morning and decided that she was keeping the baby; she was planning on telling James soon but not just yet. She wanted to get used to the idea herself before telling anyone else. Annette and Daniel had finished their dinner and Daniel had thrown the crumbs out of the front door, Annette sat down for five minutes before the timer went off on the cooker to let her know that the mince pies were ready. Annette was getting their mince pies out of the oven when there was a knock at her front door, 'Daniel' she called 'can you get that for me, I have my hands full.'

'Got it mum' Daniel called back,

James had now been sitting outside Annette's house for about an hour; he had parked a few doors down as he did not want them to see his car and guess what he was up to. For the last fifteen minutes James was sure he was not the only one plucking up the courage to knock on someone's door as he had seen a black Peugeot 406 driving up and down.

James watched as Daniel came to the door of their house and threw something into the garden; as Daniel did this he noticed the black car stop to a halt a bit further up and a large man got out and made his way to their front door, he looks like a bailiff, James thought to himself, but Annette really did not come across as the type to have a bailiff at the door. Something was telling James that this visitor meant trouble and as the man knocked on Annette's door, James got out of his car slowly and quietly, mobile phone in hand just in case.

James hid around the side of another car a bit closer to the house so he could see clearly what was going on.

Daniel opened the front door, 'Dad?' he managed to stutter out, as the man pushed Daniel back into the house and slammed the door behind him.

James ran up to the front door, he could hear screaming inside and knew that none of this was good news, he dialled 999 on his mobile and asked for police, while banging on the door. No one was answering and the screaming was getting louder, the only words he could make out was Daniel screaming 'Dad no, leave mum alone'. James kicked at the front door until if finally gave way he rushed inside to find Annette on the floor in the kitchen with the bloke on top of her, Daniel was on the man's back punching him in the head and trying to pull him off his mother. 'Leave her alone, you're going to kill her.' James looked on in horror as the man had both his hands around Annette's neck, James knew he had to do something and he had to do it quick. 'Daniel move' he shouted, he quickly ran into the kitchen and grabbed the nearest thing to him, it was a kitchen chair, he swung it behind him and with all his might he brought it down on the man's head. As the man slumped to the floor James dragged Annette away from where the man's body lay and hugged her to him. Her face was blotched with tiny pinpricks of burst blood vessels, her lips were purple but she was still breathing, her eyes were closed and as Daniel came and sat beside him, hugging and crying over his mother's limp body, James put one arm around Daniel and pulled him close. As the sirens of police cars came to a stop outside the house, five policemen came in the already broken door and as Daniel and James tried to explain what had happened they slapped a pair of hand cuffs on the unconscious man on the floor, and dragged him outside to the waiting van.

The man was indeed Daniel's father, the paramedics quickly followed inside and while James was explaining what had happened to the police, Annette was given oxygen and was loaded into the back of the waiting ambulance. The police assured James and Daniel that they would stay in the house while waiting for someone to come and fix the front door. James and Daniel had one more stop to make before they could follow the ambulance. Annette's parents had to be told, the policeman had offered to send an officer around to break the news to them, but James had insisted he was fine to tell them and besides Daniel could probably do with his grandparents right now. As they knocked on the front door, Annette's mother opened it, when she saw them at the door she knew it was bad news. Daniel rushed to his grandmother and between sobs managed to tell her, 'Dad turned up - Mum in hospital,' Josie looked at James. One look at James's ashen, tear stained face told her it was true. 'Frank! quick, our baby girl, get your shoes, car keys, whatever, we need to go see her.' Frank appeared in the doorway already pulling on his coat and slipping his feet into his shoes. 'Let's go' he commanded.

'I will follow you' said James to Annette's parents as they jumped into their car with Daniel.

Chapter Thirty Nine

When they all made it to the hospital, they were all updated by the doctor who had assessed Annette on her arrival; she had come round in the ambulance asking for Daniel. The ambulance paramedics had told her he was with her partner and they were on their way to the hospital 'Where's Simon?' The ambulance paramedics had told her he had been arrested unconscious at the scene. Annette started crying and she heard her dad's voice telling her she was safe now. Annette's parents and Daniel went into see Annette and James waited outside, he did not even know if Annette wanted to see him again. After her parents and Daniel had gone in, James paced up and down the hallway, for what felt like hours before her parents and Daniel came back out, 'she wants to see you,' her father told him, 'thank you, you saved her life,' and Frank put his arms around James and patted him on the back as James pulled away and went into the room Annette looked so small and fragile on the big white bed, she had drips in her arms and the oxygen mask on her face, he sat down on the bed next to her and held her hand, she took the oxygen mask off and whispered sorry to him as a cascade of tears spilled down her face and James had to wipe a few of his own away, they were keeping Annette in overnight for observation, but she should be home either tomorrow or Monday. 'Can James come back with us?' Daniel asked his grandparents.

'Of course he can, if he wants to.' Josie said looking at James.

'Yes thank you that would be nice.'

As James, Annette's parents and Daniel went back to Annette's parent's home, James offered to stop by the house to check all was ok before meeting them after at their house.

As James pulled up he could see the door was fixed, he parked up his car and knocked on the door, as he looked around he noticed Simon's car was still parked where he had left it almost outside Annette's house. A policeman opened the door, it was the same policeman that had been there when James had left, 'how is she?' was the first thing the policeman had asked. 'She will be ok, bruised and sore but alive thank God.'

'It's just a good thing you showed up when you did mate or this could have been a murder enquiry.'

'I know' mumbled James as the tears threatened to roll down his face once more. 'I have just come back to get a few things for her, she wanted a change of clothes and her handbag.'

'Is this her handbag?' Said the policeman holding up a black handbag from where he had unhooked it from the bottom of the banister opposite the front door.'

'Yes I think that's it, how did you know it was there?'

'It is where my wife leaves hers all the time mate' laughed the policeman handing the bag over to James. James quickly looked inside the bag to check the things Annette had asked for were in there: Keys-yes, Purse-yes, they were the two main things. James did not want to go through Annette's handbag anymore so he zipped it up and placed it down by the front door so he would not forget it. Annette had asked for something comfortable to wear and her mobile phone. James did not have a clue about which clothes to take Annette so he was going to ask Annette's mother to pick something out for her and James really did not want to go through Annette's underwear either. Annette's mobile phone was in the coat pocket, where Annette said it would be; he grabbed the phone and coat and left her house. On his way out of the door with the policeman, James remembered the car. 'When do you think you could get his car moved from over there?' asked James pointing at the black Peugeot 'We have the tow truck booked in to pick it up tonight mate. Don't worry it will be gone by the time she comes home, *if* she comes home.' The policeman said.

James asked him what he meant by *if* she comes home.

'Look mate to be honest, if one of your ex partners had tried to murder you on your kitchen floor would you want to come back in to that house again?'

'True, I never thought of it like that,' James replied then went quiet.

'I had better be off' James eventually said finally breaking the silence, 'her parent's and her son are waiting for me to come over.'

'That poor kid, we can organise counselling for him if need be. Just let us know mate, that's really something *no* kid needs to see in his or her lifetime, his own father trying to kill his mum.' The policeman shook his head as he remembered the scene he had witnessed when he had first entered the house.

James along with the policeman, left the house, said goodbye to one another and James made his way back to Annette's parent's house.

Chapter Forty

James had got in his car and was driving back to Annette's parents house when a mobile phone rang, realising it was Annette's phone he pulled over in the car to answer it.

'Maddie, are you still there? are you ok?' James had just explained everything to a shocked Maddie and was met with silence, followed by a sobbing noise.

'The bastard! The absolute sodding, arsehole, wanker' Maddie added in between sobs 'Poor Daniel. How is he?'

'Shaken up, scared, confused', I am just on my way over there now, only trouble is' confessed James 'I am a bit lost.'

'I'm on my way I will meet you there.' Maddie said as she hung up the phone after giving James directions to the house. James sat in his car for a few more minutes and composed himself before driving off again.

'James and Maddie are here' announced Daniel as he left the front room and opened the front door to them both, he flung himself into Maddie's arms and they both held on to each other.

'I could kill the bastard for what he has done to my girl,' Frank was saying between gritted teeth as they ran through the events of what had happened and they filled James in on Annette's past and how she had filed for divorce, which only made James feel worse as if it had not been for him, she may not have filed for divorce and none of this would have happened. 'You make her happy, it's not your fault' said Annette's mother as if reading James' thoughts. 'Does anyone mind if I go and see Annette?' Maddie asked.

'Of course not,' Annette's parents replied.

'I don't think I could drive, would you mind taking me?' Maddie asked James.

'No, not at all, you can take her in her handbag and coat. She wanted some comfortable clothes but I did not know what to bring.'

'No probs. We can stop off at mine and I can run in and get her a few bits of mine. Ready?' Maddie asked James.

'I just want to say goodbye to Daniel.' He left the kitchen table where they had all been sitting and walked into the front room where Daniel had been watching TV while the adults had chatted in the kitchen. James walked in and looked on the sofa, Daniel was asleep curled up. James walked over and tucked Daniel up on the sofa with a blanket he had found on the chair. Maddie felt her eyes filling with tears as she looked on silently, James would make a good dad she thought to herself.

After saying goodbye to Annette's parents James and Maddie got in James's car; after a short stop at Maddie's, where she grabbed a velour tracksuit, a change of underwear and a pair of pyjamas for Annette, they arrived at the hospital. It was gone 9 pm when they got there, visiting hours were over but they were both allowed in just for a short time. James waited outside while Maddie went in, he decided three might be a crowd so he got himself a coffee from one of the machines out in the main corridor and sat in the lounge room.

'Are you awake?' whispered Maddie as she walked into Annette's hospital room. She sat down on the chair and held her head in her hands and cried when she saw Annette; when she opened her eyes she saw Annette was awake and had tears pouring from her face too as she sat on the bed and held Maddie's hands in her own, Annette whispered;

'I lost the baby, you were right. I was pregnant.'

'Oh Annette I am so sorry.'

Annette struggled to sit upright; they wrapped their arms around each other and held on tight. 'Does James know?' asked Maddie, as they both stopped crying. Annette sadly shook her head. I only found out on Thursday, took a test, they told me about two hours ago, did not even realise I was bleeding, they took me for a scan and it was gone.'

'I need to tell James,' whispered Annette after a while, 'I need to tell him the truth, like I should have done in the first place.'

'He's waiting outside, do you want me to send him in?' Maddie asked.

'He came with you?'

'He gave me a lift, I was in no fit state to drive myself, I only just about made it to your parents.'

'How are they and how's Daniel?'

'Your parents are angry and your dad wants to kill Simon for what he has done to you.'

'They arrested him for attempted murder you know.'

'I know' nodded Maddie.

'Annette would like to see you' Maddie told James as she walked in the lounge room where James was staring at a blank TV screen. 'It helps if the TV is actually turned on to watch it you know' Maddie said to James.

'What, yes I know, could not work out how to turn the damn thing on, sorry, was in my own little world, she wants to see me?'

'Yes, go on, I will wait here for you.'

James took a deep breath and walked into the room, Annette was sitting up in bed and motioned to James to sit next to her on the bed. James did what she asked and sat on the bed next to her.

'I am your boss.'

'I lost our baby.'

'Pardon?' they both said at once.

'I am sorry, I lost our baby.'

'I never knew.'

'I only found out two days ago, I never got a chance to tell you.'

James sat in stunned silence. Annette wiped away her tears with the corner of the bed sheet.

'What do you mean you're my boss?'

James explained to Annette, that his parents owned Carrington's and how he was the boss and explained all about changing his surname to Harrington so no one would put two and two together. When James had finally explained all to Annette she sat back on the bed and whispered:

'It looks like we both hid our past from each other.'

'It does, doesn't it,' James agreed, he looked at Annette.

'I love you' he finally blurted out, 'come and live with me, you me and Daniel and I promise no one will ever harm you or Daniel again.'

'I love you too but we can't come and live with you, you are not suited for parenthood, your flat is too perfect and you only drive a two seater car, and I don't have a dog' laughed Annette which turned into a cough, which caused one of the passing nurses, to come in and give Annette a few sips of water and turn the oxygen mask back on.

'I am sorry Ms. Johnson needs her rest now said the nurse to James, 'You can come back tomorrow.'

'Ok' replied James 'Can I have five more minutes to say goodbye please'

'Five minutes' agreed the nurse as she walked back out of the room.

'I have a house.' James told Annette. When Annette did not reply, he continued, 'That's why we had an emergency meeting the other day at work when I came in, with Tom and the other man.'

The meeting was only yesterday but it felt like days ago, so much had happened since then.

'I was supposed to be selling the house to the man who was with me and Tom, but I told them the house was not for sale.'

'Why?' Annette asked.

'The more I went to the house, the more I could picture you and Daniel in the house with me, living as a family with a *real* dog running around the garden.'

Annette closed her eyes, she was suddenly quite exhausted. James noticed and stood up to leave, kissing Annette gently on her forehead, 'Think about it' he whispered to her, 'Please.'

'I will' she murmured back.

By the time James made it home it was almost midnight. Maddie had rung Annette's parents to say Annette was feeling a bit better and was now asleep. She also let them know James was going to give her a lift home and she would get a taxi over to theirs in the morning to pick up her car.

Chapter Forty One

It was now Monday afternoon, James was picking Annette up from the hospital where she was now being discharged; as James led Annette outside, towards the car park, Annette looked around before frowning and turning to James:

'Where is your car?'

'It's there' James said pointing at a silver car in the car park.

'That's not your car.'

'It is my car' he replied unlocking the car and holding the door open for Annette. She got in the car without saying a word. James shut her door and put her belongings in the boot. As he got in the driver's side Annette turned and looked in the back of the car.

'It has seats in the back.'

'Yes, saloon cars do have seats in the back, it's known as a "family car".' answered James as he started the car.

'But how, why, I' James cut her off mid sentence, 'was it not you who told me that a two seater car was not a suitable car for a family?'

'Yes, but.'

'Now will you realise how serious I am about you and Daniel. I love you Annette, and Daniel. I want you both to be in my life forever, marry me?'

Annette spluttered and took a sip from the bottle of water she had been holding on her lap.

'Did you just ask me to marry you?'

'Why yes, I believe I just did' grinned James.

Epilogue

'Mum,' 'mum,' 'mumeeee,' Annette opened one eye; 'cuggle mum cuggle' said a little voice next to her bed.

Annette sighed and lifted her two year old up in to her bed, she glanced at the clock 4.22am, another broken night's sleep.

Chloe her daughter was really starting to make a habit of this!

Every night for the last six weeks this had been happening.

Her daughter snuggled down under the covers, Annette looked at her daughter and felt a rush of love, no matter how many times Chloe woke up in the middle of the night Annette never really minded the extra little person in her bed, she loved having her baby in her arms and wondered as she stroked her daughter's soft, ringleted fair hair why babies ever had to grow up.

She heard a snore gently rise from her husband who was as he always was sound asleep unaware that they had a bed-crasher again that night.

BEEP, BEEP, BEEP, BEEP, 'Oh no is it really morning time already' groaned Annette.

'Yup it sure is 7am' came the perky response from her husband James.

'Dan!' Annette called out softly as Chloe started to wake up, lying in the crock of Annette's arm which was now dead and full of pins and needles,

'Dan!'

She called him again louder this time as she swung her legs out of bed with Chloe in one arm (the non-dead arm).

'Time to get up lazy bones you have school,'

'Yes mum,' came the muffled reply from Daniel's bedroom.

She knew he was still in bed but would appear downstairs in about half an hour in a mad rush to get to school on time.

He would give her a kiss on the cheek; grab a cake and a packet of crisps, which he classed as breakfast, completely ignoring the toast and cereal on the table, he would dash out the front door ready to meet his friends, returning two minutes later having forgotten one thing or another!

How could a group of boys, sorry, teenagers, turn what should be a twenty minute walk to school into a forty five Minute walk to school was beyond her.

She was not even going to waste her breath telling him again how if he met his friends just a little bit later he would have time for a proper breakfast and would still be able get to school on time.

'Bye mum, bye dad' Daniel called as Annette watched him join up with his friends and she smiled to herself, Daniel was a good boy and even though he was now almost sixteen years old and in his final year of secondary school, they still had a strong mother and son bond, thank goodness no one had ever ruined that. If anything they had bonded closer together, through the years all they'd had was each other, through the good times, the bad times and the darn right ugly times, which were now thankfully well and truly behind them.

Annette tidied up the kitchen after Daniel had left, making two more cups of tea.

She kissed her husband goodbye as he went off to work.

Annette sipped her own tea which was now only just warm and watched her daughter eating her breakfast, and smiled to herself. She thought about her past and frowned, she still had bad dreams every now and again but they were getting less frequent. Her life had now changed so very much for the better, she smiled again and relaxed, her mobile phone beeped *love you* the message simply read, *I love you too James* she typed back in.

message sent.

I would like to thank you all for purchasing and reading my first novel, I would also love to receive any feedback.

Please check out my website for news on my latest novels, release dates, special offers and to leave feedback

"Starting Again".

www.cjayebooks.co.uk